On Woden's Hill

AN ALNMOUTH
STORY

John Wheatley

Cover Design - Boyana
Borisova

Silversea Books

Silversea Books

Contents

1

〜

'We rode to Alnmouth, a small seaport town famous for all kinds of wickedness.' JOHN WESLEY, 19th July 1748

'Alnmouth,' said Robert, 'is such a boring place.'

'You didn't always say that,' replied Vicky, his younger sister. 'You used to talk about it all through the year. Making plans. *When we go to Alnmouth again...* you never stopped going on about it.'

It was true. Inside, Robert admitted it. Since the age of six or seven, Alnmouth had been his dream place. Even when they went abroad where it was always sunny, nothing compared with Alnmouth. Now, aged fourteen, he was disillusioned. And it didn't help when Vicky reminded him of his former enthusiasm. It just made it worse.

He glanced towards Lucy, Vicky's friend who had come on the holiday with them. She was sitting in the corner looking out of things and sorry for herself, as usual. Perhaps if Lucy wasn't there it wouldn't be so bad. She took all the fun out of it. She took all the fun out of Vicky too, which amounted to the same thing. When they were last here, two years ago, it hadn't mattered that Vicky was a girl, or that she was younger than him; they made up stories together and acted them out. Not just Alnmouth – Alnwick Castle, Dunstanburgh Castle, Craster, Lindisfarne. Now it had all gone flat. Like a hot-air balloon with no hot air, sinking to earth, its canvas crumpling up and wrinkling.

'Let's go for a walk on the beach at least,' said Vicky.

Shrugging, Robert got up and reluctantly, led the way. Vicky and

Lucy followed behind him. He didn't even turn or slow down to let them catch up with him. Guiltily, he knew they were as miserable as he was. But he couldn't help it. Or help them.

His parents had driven to Alnwick where they were curating an exhibition of paintings and other art works. His dad, of course, came from Alnwick originally and still had contacts. Whenever they were there, his dad's accent changed, reverting to the original Northumberland twang. It was something that he and Vicky used to laugh about and imitate. His dad was the organiser of the Art exhibition. Some of his mum's paintings, naturally, had crept into the display. That was the main reason why they had come to Alnmouth in the first place if the truth be told. 'Won't it be great to go back there again,' they said, when what they really meant was, 'Won't it be great for *us!*' 'We'll only need to pop in there once or twice,' they said. In fact, they had been there more or less every day because of one glitch or another.

And then, too, there was Lucy. Sad, glum, homesick Lucy, who had somehow managed to get herself included, and who obviously hated every minute of it.

'She's so wet!' Robert had confided to his mother, when she confronted him with something unkind he had said to Lucy. 'Such a pain. She drags everything down.'

His mother had taken him to one side in that serious way she had when she was appealing to his supposed grown-up status. He had been put on special behaviour to be nice to her. 'There are problems at home,' his mum said. 'That's why she came with us. She's upset. We need to be kind to her.'

He hated the way that being the eldest put this kind of responsibility on him. As if his personal behaviour could influence the outcome.

They made their way down past the corner of the golf links and along the short path, lined with sea grass, which led to the beach. The links ran parallel to the beach in a narrow strip, and above, the land rose steeply, eighty or ninety feet, to a kind of bluff, thick with vegetation. Dad had said the golf course continued up there further on, but they had never walked above the village on that side.

As they walked along towards the mouth of the river, he could hear, behind, Lucy talking about her horse. It seemed, to Robert, that that was all she ever talked about. She didn't really have a horse of her own, but went to a local stables for riding lessons, and talked about one of the horses there as if it was her own. 'I so miss Jimmy Jilkes,' she would, say, for the hundredth time. Jimmy Jilkes! It seemed like a stupid name for a horse, thought Robert.

It was a bright day with high white clouds against a blue sky but enough wind to give a fresh feeling to the air. They came to the 'ferry' which was the name his dad gave to the place where the river began to flow into the sea. In the old days - in other words when his grandmother was still young, dad had explained - there was a regular ferry boat here, rowing people across for sea bathing, and people still just called it the ferry. The tide was coming in, so that you could still see the steep sides of the channel through which the River Aln flowed out of its estuary. At the lowest tide it was easy to walk across to the other side, but you had to be careful when the tide was full, especially when it was just beginning to ebb as it created strong currents that flowed out to the sea. Across the estuary, on its sandy hill was the cross that marked the church which had once stood there; beyond that the sandy shore could be seen running on for miles and miles, into the distance, white sand, with grassy dunes behind.

The estuary curved away from the sea, going behind the village on the other side, so that Alnmouth itself was like a headland with the sea on one side and the river on the other. On the sheltered side, some boats were moored in the shallow water, or on the shelving sands. They were small boats, some with cabins, some sailing boats with masts, standing on their stilt-like keels, some with fishing tackle in them, and some which were just simple rowing boats. Higher up, above the water line, were some broken lobster pots, and a rowing boat which had been pulled up there because its wooden planks were rotten and broken. Robert couldn't remember if it had been here last time they came, but there had been others, tied up and seemingly abandoned; he had once wondered if it would be possible to save up and buy an old rowing boat, and mend it until it was seaworthy again, and he had shared this plan with Vicky, but nothing had come of it, and he could see now that it was probably just childish.

'What is Alnmouth for?' asked Lucy suddenly, as if something had just happened to make her think of the question.

Robert gave out a sigh, not bothering to attempt an answer.

'It's for people to come on holiday to,' replied Vicky.

It was the obvious answer, thought Robert, though there must have been something here before tourists started coming. Maybe just fishermen.

'It was probably just a fishing village before,' he said.

Lucy smiled, as if she was glad that he had taken the trouble to speak to her, and it made him feel guilty. After all, it wasn't so difficult to be nice to someone if you chose to.

They went back to the cottage. It was down one of the alleyways that ran, quite crookedly, from the street which formed the centre of the village. There were some new buildings and extensions in the village, some that looked a bit older and grander, as if they had been built as villas or guesthouses; some, like the cottage they were in seemed much older and as if they had been converted from another use they had once had. At the highest point of the village - with a view over both the seaward side and the estuary - was the friary.

'Is a friary the same as a monastery?' Vicky had once asked.

'Similar,' their dad replied. 'But it's more a place people go to for retreats these days.'

'What's a retreat?'

'Where people go for a bit of peace and quiet, basically.'

Robert sat in the main room, switched on the TV, and flicked through a few channels. Vicky and Lucy went up to the room they were sharing. Robert settled on a cartoon programme, and watched it, though he also felt annoyed with himself because he didn't really want to watch it at all.

'Look what we've found,' announced Vicky, coming into the doorway with Lucy at her shoulder. She waited for Robert to show interest, and then, when he didn't, she carried on, 'we've found a tent.'

Almost against his wishes, Robert turned to look. Vicky was holding an orange sausage shaped bag, with obvious tent poles sticking out of one end. It was the kind of discovery which, in the old days, would have set both of them into a rush of excitement and imaginary adventures.

'Shall we put it up outside?' Vicky asked.

There was a small patch of grass just under the kitchen window.

'Are there any pegs?'

'I think so. There's something that feels like a bag of metal pegs.'

'Go on, then,' said Robert trying not to break his image of being bored and fed-up with everything. Reluctantly, he followed them outside, and once there took charge, as they obviously expected, of the putting up of the tent.

'What's that?' asked mum when they came back in.

'We found it in a cupboard in our room,' Vicky answered. 'Can we sleep in it tonight, just me and Lucy, just in the yard here I mean?'

'Has it got a groundsheet?' asked dad.

Robert knew from the start that they would not be allowed to sleep out, but that rather than say so outright, dad would find a way of working round to the point where you could see for yourself that it just wasn't sensible. You could save yourself a lot of time by just working it out for yourself.

The tent didn't have a groundsheet.

'But does it have to have one? The grass is quite dry.'

'It might be now, but in the morning, with the dew and everything...'

'Couldn't we make something out of bin-liners?'

It went on for some time before it ended in exactly the way Robert had predicted. Vicky was disappointed.

Lucy, he sensed, was not.

They had brought pizzas from Alnwick and when they had been heated up in the oven, they all sat round the table.

'Can we go somewhere tomorrow for a change?' Robert asked. 'Dunstanburgh Castle or Warkworth?'

'Can we,' echoed Vicky.

'We can...' mum began, 'but not tomorrow. The day after, yes.

Promise. Tomorrow we just have a little bit more work to finish and then it will be done.'

Mum sounded bright and breezy, but you could tell she felt guilty about it underneath. Robert wanted to make some comment that would underline it, something sarcastic, but he knew that could lead to a row and that he would then be in danger of putting himself in the wrong. He chose to remain silent.

'So,' said mum, the following morning, as they sat having breakfast, 'what are you three going to do today?'

'Don't know,' said Vicky, glumly, 'probably walk down to the beach again.'

'Don't worry, mum,' Robert said, in a positive tone that he had been preparing, 'we'll find something to keep us busy.'

Mum looked at him in a slightly odd way, but then decided to accept it. 'Good!' she said. 'And tomorrow, we'll drive up to Seahouses and have fish and chips, how's that?'

'Fine,' said Robert.

'Fine,' the girls echoed.

All settled.

'Right,' said Robert when mum and dad had set off in the car towards Alnwick. 'Here's what we are going to do...' The idea had come to him in the night, and he had deliberately not told Vicky in case she blurted it out... 'we're going to take the tent over to Woden's Hill.'

'What's that?' asked Lucy.

'The hill with the cross on.'

'I thought it was called Church Hill...'

'It is. But dad said it used to be a pagan temple.'

'Woden's Hill. Sounds spooky.'

'You mean we're going across the ferry?'

'Yes, across the ferry. We'll take some food, put the tent up and have a picnic. Then, if we want, we can walk along the beach to Warkworth. It's not too far.'

Vicky looked interested. Lucy looked alarmed. 'Will it be dangerous?' she asked.

'Course not,' said Robert. He knew it wouldn't be dangerous. It wasn't even all that exciting really, but the idea had just brought back a little bit of the spirit of adventure he and Vicky used to share. In the old days, they would just have made it up as they went along. But anyway, it was something their parents would absolutely have forbidden and in that lay some of its appeal.

'What about the tide?' asked Vicky, who knew all the warnings there were about the dangers of the tide in the estuary channel.

'I've checked,' said Robert. 'It's low tide in about twenty minutes. Just enough time for us to get ready. I'll pack the tent. You two get some food.'

Vicky was now getting that look on her face that meant she was keen. Lucy was still looking anxious.

'We'll have fun,' said Robert, giving her a little play punch on the shoulder. 'Better than just walking around again.'

It was enough to draw Lucy, however reluctantly, into the slipstream.

2

It was just as Robert predicted. The channel between the steep banks was just a shallow babbling stream, quite wide, but nothing at all like the swollen flood it became when the tide flowed out of the estuary. Even Lucy was reassured, as she took off her shoes and socks in preparation to paddle across. It was quite easy, but you just needed to concentrate where there were slippery stones.

'Watch out for crabs!' called Robert.

Vicky squealed with laughter. Lucy redoubled her concentration.

On the other side, they walked across the sandy shore. At the foot of the hill with the cross, the hill which Robert had decided now to call Woden's Hill, there was a stone wall, like a belt holding the hill in. They scrambled past this and clambered up the slope towards the cross.

'There used to be a pagan temple and then a church here,' Robert explained. 'I remember dad telling me. It was part of the village then, and then something happened, and it diverted the river to where it now is, and this became cut off. So, they had to build another church in the village. It was ages ago.'

They put up the tent on the sheltered side of the hill facing away from the village and then looked around. It was still possible to find the stumps of wall where the old church had been.

'What now?' said Vicky when they had finished exploring. She was looking to Robert to continue the adventure.

'We'll take our picnic and begin to walk along towards Warkworth.'

'Aren't we going to have the picnic where the tent is?'

Robert thought for a moment. He had to admit that it was pretty pointless having the tent if they weren't going to use it.

'The tent is just our base camp,' he said. 'The place where we made our landfall.'

Neither of the girls seemed to want to risk asking what a landfall was, but the idea of having a base camp, seemed, for some reason, acceptable.

'What about the tide for going back?' asked Lucy.

'What?'

'Won't it be full later on?'

Robert was a little annoyed by all the questions. 'It'll be back out again later,' he said. 'Obviously,' he added, though admitting to himself that he had been less precise about checking the time of the afternoon tide. 'But anyway,' he went on, 'if need be, we can always walk the long way, round the other side of the estuary as far as the bridge, and then come back into the village that way.'

This seemed to bring some reassurance.

They walked for a time, and then found a sort of sheltered recess in the sand dunes where they stopped for their picnic.

'Sausage rolls and lemonade,' said Vicky, 'just like the Famous Five.'

'Did they have sausage rolls?' asked Lucy.

'Probably not,' said Robert. 'Who cares!'

'We're the Famous Three,' said Lucy, and for almost the first time in the holiday there seemed to be a hint of fun in her voice.

They finished their picnic and walked on.

'The sky is changing,' said Vicky, not long after they had set out.

'What?'

'Look. Back in the direction we've come from.'

They all turned. It was true. Above Woden's Hill and the village, now small in the distance, a bank of darker sky seemed to be rising, almost as if it were being drawn up like a blind.

'We'd better get back,' ordered Robert. 'It looks as if it's a storm brewing. He strode forward, leading the way. The bank of darkness now began to advance more quickly, covering half the sky, until it was above them, and stretching all the way from the land to the sea horizon. There was a flicker of sheet lightning and ten seconds later a distant rumble of thunder.

'That means it's two miles away,' said Robert. 'We should be able to get to the tent.'

A patter of rain now began.

I bet it's not waterproof,' said Vicky.

'You were the one who wanted to sleep out in it last night,' Robert retorted.

'I wish we'd stayed at home,' said Lucy, sounding fretful.

Robert dropped back and put his arm round her shoulder. 'It's all right,' he said. 'Nothing to worry about. And if nothing else, the tent will give us a bit of shelter, a temporary reprieve.'

Again, he stepped on ahead, setting the pace. *A temporary reprieve,* he thought to himself, pondering the phrase, *I wonder where I got that from, must be something I read in a book.*

A fork of lightning broke from the sky, seeming to hit the sea just on the horizon. Robert counted: 1... 2... 3... 4... 5... then came the expected roll of thunder, nearer, angrier. One mile. He decided not to say anything. He turned to wait for Vicky and Lucy to catch him up. Looking down the coast, the whole sky was now dark, masking the distance in a cloak of inky fog.

Suddenly the rain redoubled, stippling the sand like a volley of bullets, and they began to run.

At last, they reached the tent, and Vicky and Lucy crawled inside.

'I'll just check the pegs and the guy ropes are all right,' said Robert, and then, when this was done, 'Hutch up a bit in there. Make room for me.'

They sat, all three, crouching in the tent, water steaming down their faces.

'At least it's dry in here, after all,' said Vicky, and then let out an unintentional bubble of a giggle.

'Try not to touch the canvas,' said Robert, seriously. 'That might draw the water through.'

Vicky giggled again.

'What are you laughing at?' said Robert, sternly, unimpressed.

'Well, it's just...' again she had to forcefully stop a giggle, 'well, it's just that we're already soaked through to the skin, so it hardly seems to matter.'

This, Robert ignored.

'What about lightning?' asked Lucy, in a very little voice, almost like an apology for being bold enough to say anything at all.

'How do you mean?'

'Might not the lightning strike the tent poles?'

'No,' said Robert, decisively. 'If anything, it will hit the cross. That's higher up.'

As a matter of fact, Robert was not very sure if this was the case or not, but he decided not to say anything that might undermine his own authority.

Chapter 3

3

~

It was nearly an hour later that the ferocity of the rain began to abate. The worst of the storm now seemed to have passed over. Popping his head out of the tent, Robert saw that the sky was still murky, the sea dark and troubled.

'We'll give it another ten minutes,' he announced. 'Then we'll make our way back.'

'What about the tent?' asked Vicky.

'Leave it here, for the time being, anyway, just in case.'

Neither of the girls asked *in case of what?* They seemed content to leave it to Robert's authority.

'Right,' he said, at last. 'It's eased off now, let's go.'

One by one they came out of the cramped tent. There was still a mist, like low cloud, swirling around, obscuring the view.

'Look,' said Lucy, suddenly.

'What?'

'It's different.'

Lucy was looking up to where the large cross, so clearly visible from the village, had been. It was no longer there.

'It must have blown down in the storm,' said Vicky.

'No, it's not just that,' Lucy replied. 'Look.'

A little further on, the walls of a ruin stood, like broken teeth; a ruin, but still one which had the shape of a church. Both girls looked towards Robert, as if they trusted him to have an explanation, but he, too, looked completely flummoxed.

'Never mind that,' he said at last. 'It doesn't matter. Let's just get back, see what state the tide is in.'

'We don't need to worry about the tide,' said Vicky, as they came round the side of the hill.

They all looked down.

'Where's the river gone?' said Lucy.

The channel of the river, which had been so clear even at low tide, was simply not there. Instead, the beach now curved round onto a meadow sparsely covered with rough sea grass, rising to the bank of the estuary; the river, it appeared now flowed round the other side of Woden's Hill. Beyond, the village itself was still veiled in low sea mist.

'Let's get across, anyway,' said Robert. 'You never know...'

They scrambled down the hill to the level, and then, looking both to the right and to the left as if they were about to cross a busy road, they picked their way nimbly across, and began to make their way to the corner of the village.

The mist was beginning to dissolve by now and the outline of the buildings at the bottom of the village was emerging. As they made their way forward, they saw that the way was blocked by a group of children, five or six of them, standing together, watching their approach. Robert stopped and signalled to Vicky and Lucy to wait just behind him. He could not make out whether the children, mostly younger than themselves, were just curious or actually hostile.

Then, as they stood off, one of the group - a stocky lad who might have been the same age as Robert - pointed towards them and began to laugh, a harsh mocking cackle of a laugh, and as he continued to point, he looked sideways to the others, urging them to join in, which, once they sensed there was no danger, they did.

'What's the matter with them? Idiots!' exclaimed Vicky.

All the children were now laughing and pointing, sounding like a gaggle of geese.

'It's our clothes,' said Lucy. 'They're laughing at our clothes.'

'I don't see why,' retorted Vicky. 'We may look bedraggled but they look as if they're going to a fancy dress party!'

'No,' said Robert, who had stayed silent through this. 'Not fancy dress. That's what they wear. Don't you see, they're wearing clothes from a different time. We must be in another time dimension. That's why the ruin of the church is there. That's why the ferry has disappeared.'

Before either of the girls could question him on this, another member of the group, this time a smaller boy, with a ragged shirt and a pinched dirty face, had stepped to one side and picked up a stone which he hurled towards them. Luckily his aim was not good, and the stone went skittering off the pebbles at the top of the beach, but his boldness was a signal to several of the others, who now seemed intent on following his example.

At this point, however, another person broke through the group from behind, a girl looking to be about the same age as Robert, and in an angry voice, she warned them off, threatening what she would do to them if they didn't cut it out. Her words seemed to be aimed pointedly at the stocky lad who looked cowed by her, and once he took to his heels, the rest followed quickly after.

The little group of three now found themselves looking at the girl, and it was clear that - though she had done them a favour in coming to their rescue - she was as puzzled by their appearance as the others had been.

Robert stepped forward and made a little polite bow.

'Thank you,' he said. 'We are very grateful.'

'Who are you?' asked the girl. 'Where are you from?'

Her accent was like the locals they had heard in Alnmouth, but much stronger, so much so that it was difficult at first to make out her words.

Not knowing what else to say, Robert pointed back to the hill. 'From the church,' he said. 'We were just trying to cross the river, you see and...' At this point, he seemed to run out of explanation, and simply shrugged his shoulders and made an open gesture with his hands.

The girl stared at them a moment longer, and then made a decision. 'You'd better come with me, quick like, before you're seen by anyone else.'

She turned, and without further words, led the way, choosing the little alleyways and narrow lanes to take them wherever it was she was taking them to.

'All the buildings are different,' whispered Lucy. She had noticed this at first from the beach but had been too preoccupied with the hostility of the children to say anything.

'It's weird,' said Vicky.

'It's what I said,' replied Robert. 'It is weird. But it must mean we have somehow broken out of the time continuum.'

'What's *the time continuum*?' asked Vicky.

'Well, normally time just goes forward, right? So, if we are now in the past, something's gone wonky. Somehow, we must have crossed over into a different time.'

'How can we have done that?'

'I don't know. It's something I used to imagine, but I don't know how it could actually happen. It must be something to do with the storm.'

'Can't we just go back and make it unhappen?' said Vicky.

'I don't know. Maybe we should just go along with it. See what happens.'

They had now arrived at a small courtyard, from which a narrow path led between two buildings. At the end of the path was another yard, and now the girl stopped and, opening a door, ushered them into a dark space which smelled of straw and farm animals.

She turned to them. 'My name is Anna,' she said. 'You will be safe here for a time. The children think I am a witch, and, you heard me, I threatened to put a curse on anyone of them who tells tales.'

'What about the bigger lad?' asked Robert.

'Matty. My cousin. He is afraid of me too, because of tales I can tell of him, mind you.'

'What if anyone else saw us?'

'People were sheltering from the storm. In the alehouses mainly where they will no doubt bide a while. I think no-one saw you.'

'But we can't stop here forever, can we,' said Lucy.

'Maybe we should just go, before they come out of the pub,' suggested Vicky.

'You can go, if you like,' said Anna, 'but first I will find you some proper clothes. You can't go anywhere looking like that.'

4

They waited for Anna to return. As their eyes adjusted to the gloom, they saw that they were in a long room, with straw on the floor, and some bales on which they found a place to sit. At the far end was a pen which led to an enclosed space outside where a goat was tethered. There were also a few hens, and a cat, who was too shy to come near them, but who occasionally made a dart to catch something. 'Rats probably,' thought Robert, though knowing Vicky's feelings about rats, he decided to keep it quiet.

'How long do you think she'll be?' asked Lucy.

'No idea,' Robert replied. 'We'll just have to trust her.'

'It's a bit stinky in here, isn't it?' remarked Vicky.

They sat for a time, lost in their own thoughts.

'Do you think we'll have to wear the same clothes she does?' asked Lucy, at last.

'Probably.'

They pictured the long woollen skirt, the thick cotton smock, the shawl, the white apron and headscarf.

'I think it might suit Robert very well,' said Vicky, and a sudden snort of laughter bubbled from her, which nearly set Lucy off too.

'Shut up, you two,' said Robert, annoyed at their levity, but before he could say more, the door opened, and Anna came back in.

She was carrying a bundle tied in a sheet and indicated that they should follow her up the rickety staircase to a room above which contained rows of sacks.

'Grain,' she explained, as she opened up the bundle. 'This is a storehouse. Mainly for grain.'

From the sheet tumbled a variety of garments, smocks, skirts, scarfs, stockings, shawls, boots, breeches, slippers. She began to extract them, and to hand them to whoever she thought might try putting them on.

'I don't know how well they will fit,' she said. 'They're mine, mainly, but the boy's stuff is my cousin's, Matty, the one you saw, and some my uncle's.'

The girls went behind a stack of sacks, and muffled giggles could be heard as they tried things on. Robert found another place to change further down the room.

'Are you from south of here?' Anna called.

'South?'

'Ashington? Whitley Bay? That's the direction you were coming from into the village.'

'Yes,' Robert called back, vaguely, 'from the south direction.'

'They say it's warmer in the south. Sailors who've been there, I mean. That's what they say. Is that why you wear such strange clothes?'

'Well, yes,' replied Robert. 'Where we come from everyone wears clothes like these.'

'I thought so. People here are suspicious of strangers. Most people have good hearts, but they are watchful of people from outside the village. When I first came here from Alnwick, people didn't trust me. That's why some of the children believe it when I tell them I'm a witch.'

The cat, which had followed them up the stairs, was sitting on Anna's knee when the two girls emerged from their changing place. They looked quite pleased with themselves, in the way you might playing a game of dressing up.

Anna inspected them and nodded her approval, though she said to Lucy that she had to rearrange her hair, which was still hanging down from the scarf onto her shoulders. 'You can't have it like that,' she explained. 'People will think the wrong thing about you!'

'Oh!' said Lucy, beginning to blush a little. 'I didn't realise!'

A moment later, Robert came out from behind his changing place with a very self-conscious look on his face. He was wearing a smock and a waistcoat, with knee-breeches and leggings beneath.

'The trousers are too big,' he complained. 'I've got to hold them up with my hand.'

Vicky and Lucy giggled, and Robert gave them a stare. 'They're Matty's,' Anna explained, trying not to smile. 'He's much fatter than you. I'll try to find you a belt or at least some rope to tie round. And now I must go – people will be wondering where I am. I'll bring some food, and then I can help you plan how to get to wherever it is you are travelling to.'

As she stood, the cat jumped off her knee and followed her down the rickety staircase. After she had gone, they looked at one another, wearing their strange new clothes, with a look of bemusement on their faces. Then they began to laugh. Even Robert, so serious up to now, could see the funny side of it.

'But seriously,' said Vicky, when the moment of amusement had passed, 'what are we going to do?'

'We can't just stay here like this, can we?' chimed in Lucy.

'Robert?'

'I don't know. I'm thinking.'

'Well?' asked Vicky, impatiently, after she had allowed Robert a minute of thinking time.

'All I know is we were on the hill, Woden's Hill, in the tent, during the storm and when we came out, we were here.'

'And the river had changed course,' said Lucy.

'And here is not here, as it was; it looks as if it ought to be but in fact it's not,' said Vicky.

'So what does it all mean,' asked Lucy, 'that we've gone into some sort of time warp?'

'It must do. Something like that, anyway.'

'The question being, how do we get out of it again. Robert?'

'I don't know why you keep asking me.'

'Well, you always seem to know more about these things than anyone else.'

'At the present, I have to admit, I haven't the foggiest.'

'Perhaps we should just go back there, to where the tent is, and wait,'
suggested Vicky.

'Maybe if we could fall asleep or something, you know, in the tent, it
would all have changed back again when we wake up,' added Lucy.

'Like a dream?'

'Yes.'

'Only it doesn't feel at all like a dream, does it?' They all agreed that it
didn't feel like a dream.

They sat for a time in silence, with no new ideas coming forward.

'What if...' said Robert, at last, 'I know this will sound stupid, but you
know when you were younger and you played a game, and it seemed completely real, as if the boundary between your imagination and what's real
had disappeared? What about if this is just the next stage on from that?'

They gave this some serious consideration.

'But then you can just click out of it,' said Vicky. 'Mum says your tea's
ready, and you just click out of it.'

'Or like when you're reading a book,' said Lucy, coming in suddenly
with her idea. 'Sometimes when you're reading a book you really feel as if
you are one of the characters, or that you're really in the place.'

'I suppose it might just wear off,' said Vicky. 'Better keep our own
clothes with us just in case.'

On this note, which Vicky had intended as a joke, the discussion fell
silent again.

'What sort of food do you think she'll bring?' asked Lucy, changing
the subject.

'I don't know. Bread, I suppose. Maybe cheese. Maybe fish. I expect
they catch plenty of fish round here.'

'Anything will do for me,' said Robert, 'I'm absolutely starving.'

He had found a comfortable position for himself, lying across the top
of three corn sacks with his hands behind his head, and he closed his eyes
as if he was trying to get to sleep. Vicky and Lucy sat down cross-legged

and helped each other to adjust their scarves so that all the hair was taken up.

'What do you think of her?' asked Vicky. 'Of Anna, I mean.'

'She seems nice enough.'

'Yes. Not at all like you'd imagine a witch.'

'No.'

'What do you think, Robert?'

Robert simply grunted, as one who did not want his thoughts to be disturbed.

It was true, though. There was nothing about Anna that might make you think of a witch, unless you were the kind of child who would believe anything you were told. She a had a kindly face, pale, with soft brown eyes, and a wide mouth that showed nice white teeth. The little hair that showed under her scarf was dark, though it was difficult to tell exactly because most of it was covered up. She was almost as tall as Robert, but you would think, from her manner, that she was probably a year or two older.

An hour had passed before Anna returned. There was a click of the latch of the door below, and a moment of tension, fearing it might be someone else, and then Anna's face appeared at the top of the stair.

She handed a lighted candle to Robert, and then went back down, returning a moment later with a basket containing, as they had thought, bread, cheese, a little ham, some apples. She watched as they tucked in hungrily.

'I'm sorry I was so long,' she said. 'At the inn, there was some talk. Of strangers in the village after the storm. I think you need to be careful.'

'Why? If we blend in.'

'Most people know each other here, and tomorrow is market day in Amble so there will be fewer people around. Sometimes, sailors from strange parts come from the boats for the taverns. You could pretend you are with a boat, but it's better really if I just help you to get on your way. Tell me where you are going to.'

She waited for a reply but there was none.

'You can trust me.'

'It's not that, it's just...' Vicky began.

'Alnwick,' said Robert, coming in quickly. 'That's where we're going first, anyway. To see relations.'

'I'm from Alnwick. Who are your relations. Perhaps I may know them.'

'Well, the relations aren't actually in Alnwick, but that's where we are going first, that's all.'

'I will show you the best way. We can set out first thing in the morning. Before first light.'

'We know the way,' said Vicky.

Robert looked at her trying to signal to her that she was on tricky ground. But she ignored him.

'You just go over the bridge and follow the road. It's simple.'

'Bridge?' Said Anna curiously. Then she smiled. 'I know of no bridge. Who's been telling you stories?'

'The bridge...' Vicky repeated, looking to Robert for assistance.

'You're thinking of somewhere else,' he said.

'You'll need me to show you where the fording place is. You can stay on this side of the river, if you like, but it makes it a long journey, especially walking. And some of the land is marshy.'

'Right,' said Robert. 'So can we stay here tonight. I mean, can we sleep here?'

'There's a loft above here. You get into it by that ladder. I will bring some sacks and blankets, but I'll just leave them inside the door downstairs in case anyone is watching. But you will be safe up there here for tonight. It used to be a place where the watchman lodged in days gone by, but now no-one ever goes up there.'

After she had gone, they climbed up into the loft. It was musty but dry, with straw on the floor.

'I suppose it will have to do,' said Robert.

'Better than nothing.'

'For tonight anyway.'

'What about tomorrow morning though?' asked Lucy.

'Well,' said Robert, 'thanks to Vicky she thinks we are heading for Alnwick.'

'You were the one who said Alnwick!' Vicky protested.

'Only to stop you from saying what you were going to say.'

'Well,' said Vicky, defending herself, 'one of us had to say something!'

'She's going to give us the directions.'

'But there's no point in us going to Alnwick, is there?'

At this point, they seemed to have reached another dead-end, though they all agreed that it was beginning to get cold. Robert climbed down the ladder and then the staircase to the door. It was quite dark down there now, but he could see that Anna had been back, leaving, as promised, some blankets.

'Maybe we should tell her the truth,' said Vicky, when they had wrapped themselves up as snug as possible.

'Take her into our confidence.'

'She'd never believe us,' Lucy replied.

'I've just thought of something,' said Robert.

'What?'

'My mobile phone. It's in the pocket of my jeans.'

'But will it work? I mean if we are in a whatsit, a time warp thingy, will we be able to make calls or send texts?'

'I wouldn't have thought so.'

'Might be worth a go, though.'

Robert went to fetch the phone from where they had stacked their own clothes, and they gathered around his shoulders, as he switched it on.

The phone screen lit up for a moment or two then dissolved into black flickering shapes and lines.

'Well, it was worth a try, I suppose.'

Disappointed, they went back to their places. The candle burned on as darkness now filled the loft.

'It's weird, isn't it,' said Vicky. 'You always think you can just touch a switch and light will come on, but here it's totally different.'

'What are we going to do when the candle burns out? asked Lucy, with some concern in her voice.

'Hang on,' said Robert. 'I know the phone doesn't work, but the torch might.'

He switched on the phone, and tapped the phone icon, The beam of cold light spread in a cone on the floor.'

'Well, that's something.'

'OK,' said Robert, 'Now that we know we've got the light from the phone, in case of emergency, are we all agreed that we should snuff the candle and try to get some sleep?'

Taking the silence for agreement, he wet his finger and thumb, and with a little hiss, the flame was extinguished. They settled back, trying to make themselves comfortable.

'Have you thought,' said Vicky into the darkness, 'we may end up being stuck here forever?'

'There are some things I wouldn't miss,' said Lucy, quietly.

5

〜

They awoke early. The cold had penetrated their coverings, and they were stiff from lying on the hard floor.

'What are we going to do now?' asked Lucy.

'Just wait until Anna comes, I suppose.'

'Just think,' said Vicky, 'if we were at home now, I mean, you know, if we were back, we would just float downstairs, see what's in the fridge, put the kettle on, set the toaster going...'

'Stop it!' said Lucy, laughing.

'Bacon and eggs, maybe, a couple of sausages. Whatever you fancy.'

'Enough!' insisted Robert. 'You're doing my head in.'

They went down the ladder to the next floor where a small window looked out over the yard below. From the window, above other rooftops and corners of buildings, they could just make out the estuary and the masts of some ships.

'It seems familiar somehow, doesn't it?' said Vicky.

'It's just like the view from our bedroom,' said Lucy. 'Not exactly, but if you make a few allowances, it could be just the same angle.'

'Can't be, can it?' said Vicky.

Robert was looking around thoughtfully, then walking here and there as if sizing it up.

'I think Lucy could be right,' he said, at last. 'If you think about the way Anna brought us here yesterday, through that alley from the estuary. And then think of the lane we use to get back from the beach. I mean, dad always says that a lot of the buildings go back a long way in time, and that they've been altered and adapted. Well, I think this could be our cottage. Look where the door is downstairs, and the position of the staircase. Then, if you think of this space being divided into two rooms, yours, and mum and dad's, and a bathroom. And mine is the attic, only now it's got a proper staircase, and it's been made bigger, and it's got dormer windows. And there, outside, where the goat is tied up and the hens, is the garden where we put up the tent. It's our cottage, only this is what it was like then, and after that, at some point, it was converted into a proper house.'

'That's amazing,' said Vicky. 'Well spotted, Lucy.'

'Well, it was Robert really.'

'No,' said Robert, 'it was you who spotted it.'

As they pondered this new aspect of things, they heard the latch downstairs, signalling Anna's return once more.

'I'm sorry I'm so late,' she began. 'My uncle – Abel Slattery, that is - came back last night. I couldn't slip out. Here I've brought you some more food.'

She began to empty the contents of her basket.

'There's more bread. And some cooked sausages from breakfast at the inn. They're cold now, but still tasty.'

'What's this?' asked Vicky indicating a stone flagon with a cork in the top.

'It's small beer,' Anna replied.

'Beer!' retorted Vicky, shocked. 'Won't we get drunk?'

Anna laughed. 'It isn't the kind of beer strong enough to get you drunk, even children. It's better than water. Bad water can sometimes make you sick.'

They sat around on the bales and shared out the food, all agreeing that the small beer was different but quite drinkable. As they ate, the cat came out from its hiding and again settled on Anna's lap.

Finally, Robert chose the moment to begin the explanation they had discussed.

'Anna,' he began. 'We need to tell you something.'

She raised her eyebrows, waiting curiously, as Robert chose a way to begin. 'We haven't come from a different place,' he said, emphasising the word 'place'. 'We've sort of come from a different time. From a time in the future. About a couple of hundred years, I should think. Roughly, anyway.'

Anna looked at him with a blank face. It meant nothing to her at all.

'That's where our clothes come from, too,' added Lucy. 'Don't you see, that's why they're so different?'

Vicky came in enthusiastically, 'There are all sorts of things, cars, aeroplanes that fly across the sky, motorways, computers, mobile phones.'

'What are all these things? I think you're mocking me.'

'Mobile phones,' said Lucy. 'That's it. Show her the torch from your phone, Robert.'

Robert took the phone from the deep pocket he had found on the inside of his jerkin, and Anna's eyes narrowed at the strangeness of the object.

'Watch,' said Robert. 'I'll show you something.'

He touched the icon, and at the sight of the thin cone of light, Anna took in a little gasp of breath, frightened. 'Are you spirits?' she asked. 'Are you a sorcerer?' She turned to Vicky, 'Are you a sorceress? And you?'

'No,' said Lucy. 'Not at all! Please don't be frightened.'

She raised her palms offering a hug, and after a moment Anna accepted. 'We're just ordinary people just like you. Honestly.'

'Show me again.'

'Here,' said Robert. 'You hold it.'

Anna shook her head.

'It doesn't hurt,' he said. 'Just put your fingertip on this little circle.'

After a moment, she lifted her hand and touched the case of the phone with her finger, then drew her finger away hastily as if she suddenly feared it might be hot.

'It's all right,' said Robert. 'Just touch the little circle with your finger.'

She did so, and then immediately jumped back again as the cone of bluish light spread out.

They all laughed and took turns until at last Anna was persuaded to hold the phone and switch on the torch.

'I still don't understand,' she said. 'Has it got fire in it, and if it has why isn't it hot?'

'It's a bit like fire, but it's more, well, a kind of energy that's been squashed up into a tiny box, we call it a battery.'

Anna shook her head. It made no sense to her at all, but she seemed to accept that they had somehow come from another time without being sorcerers or witches or devils in disguise.

'But how did you travel?'

'That's it. We don't really know. All we know is that we were on the hill where the church is, in our own time, sheltering during the storm, and when it passed, we were here but everything had changed. That was just before we saw you yesterday. It had just happened a few minutes before.'

Anna nodded her head slowly, thoughtfully. 'It was truly a bad storm,' she said, as if thinking there might be hidden power in a storm that might bring about some kind of natural magic. 'Very unusual, even for December.'

'December?' questioned Vicky.

'Yes. People were saying that the warm weather lately would bring about no good, and so it has proved. Maybe we will get a proper winter now.'

'How come we've changed seasons as well?' asked Lucy.

'If I could answer that, I'd be a genius,' Robert retorted.

'Maybe we just got off at the wrong stop!' quipped Vicky.

As if to confirm Anna's information about the time of year, the afternoon brought a light covering of snow. From the window of the granary, they could see the soft light flakes, drifting slowly down and beginning to gather on the roof-tops; across the estuary, the sky was a dull heavy yellowish colour.

'No wonder it felt cold last night,' said Vicky.

'Probably be even colder tonight.'

6

~

As if she had sensed their concern, when Anna returned in the evening with more food in her basket, she also brought more sacks and shawls. Helping them to get arranged, she seemed to have forgotten the strangeness of their tale, and to be concentrating entirely on the practicalities of the here and now.

'Did you say you were from Alnwick?' asked Robert when they were settled.

'Yes. I came to Alnmouth a year ago, a little longer, maybe. Well, to be plain, I was sent here by my father to be the housekeeper for my uncle.'

'You say that as if it's something you didn't want,' said Lucy. Anna was quiet for a moment, seemingly in a reflective mood, and then, she continued. 'Up until my tenth birthday, nearly five years ago, I was as happy as any child could be. My father is a wine merchant, Mr Summers of Alnwick, not rich but prosperous enough, and I had more advantages than many, especially amongst the poor. Most of all, I had a kind mother, who taught me all the things I needed to know for when it was time to look after my own house. She told me stories too. She couldn't read and so she couldn't teach me that, and my father said I had no need of it, but she had lots of old stories in her memory, and she used to enthral me with her tales as we sat by the fireside in the parlour at night.

'But then she grew ill. At first, she told me it would pass in time, but after a while I could see with my own eyes that she was wasting away, and it was not many months before we were seeing her lowered into her grave.

My father was kind to me then. We had never been really close, because he was so often about his business, but for a time he looked after me and comforted me when I was full of sadness.

'I then became the keeper of the house, and I made it my business to do everything as well as my mother had done when she was alive, and I thought all was well in our house. But my father then decided to take another wife. In less than a year after my mother's death, she became my stepmother. At the beginning she pretended to fuss over me and to spoil me, but it soon became clear, to me - at least in private - that she wanted to have no other woman in the house than herself. I believe she was jealous. I heard her sometimes, when she didn't think I was close by, wheedling and cajoling my father, telling him to find a position for me where I wouldn't be in her way.'

'Did he not see how you felt?'

'When I spoke to him about it, he became silent or angry, and would avoid seeing me. She had him in her power, the way some women do have a power over men. I don't think he wanted to hurt or harm me, but at any request from me to discuss my situation, he would go into a rage. I think his anger was partly against himself, and I think that was because he felt guilty.'

'I can understand that,' said Lucy. 'Weak people get angry at their own weakness. My dad is a bit like that sometimes.'

'Sometimes, when he was in a calmer mood, he would tell me that he only had my best interests at heart, but if I said otherwise, he flew into a rage again. At last, I was told by my stepmother that I was to be sent here, to be the housekeeper of my uncle, Abel Slattery. He isn't really my uncle, but some relation of hers, a cousin or something like that, but I am sworn to call him uncle as if he were a blood relation.'

'What is he? I mean, what does he do?'

'He owns the inn you've heard me mention, which is next to here on the street. I am the housekeeper there, but also, I have to work in the inn when there is a need. There's a village girl called Dolly who is meant to do it, but she is very unreliable, always sick with one thing or another. Abel Slattery is also a merchant. He has a ship in the harbour and uses it to deliver grain to the bigger harbours on the coast. And to bring things back. Other goods. Leather. Wool. Contraband, too.'

'What is contraband?' asked Vicky.

'Smuggling,' explained Robert.

'Is he a smuggler then? That sounds quite exciting!'

'Shut up, Vicky!'

'Sorry.'

Anna continued. 'I quite liked it here at first. I had never seen the sea before, and knew nothing of it, except in tales my mother had told me, and I thought it was beautiful. So, to begin with, it was like starting a new life, and I was determined to make the best of it.'

'You lived in Alnwick, and you'd never seen the sea?' said Vicky, with disbelief.

'People don't travel unless they have to. Most people in Alnwick have never seen the sea.'

'But don't you like Alnmouth still? We've always loved it, well, Robert and me.'

'To like Alnmouth is one thing,' said Anna, in a tone that did not bode well. 'To like Abel Slattery is another.'

It was clear from her face that all was not well between her so-called uncle and herself. She maintained a pensive silence. Out of respect, the others remained silent, too.

'Is he a hard master?' said Robert, at last, quietly.

'Is he cruel to you?' came in Vicky, enthusiastic at the possibility of drama.

Anna smiled, a little wanly. 'The question is,' she said, briskly, changing the subject, 'what is to be done about you three? As you seem to have come from nowhere -from nowhere that I can understand, at least - and as you have nowhere to go to, I am at a loss to know what to suggest.'

'We need to get back to our own time,' said Vicky.

'You would be safer,' continued Anna, not responding to this, 'to leave Alnmouth and seek refuge in one of the bigger places, like Alnwick or Seahouses, where there are more people and where you can be lost in the crowd and not attract attention. It may be that we should think along those lines. I will think, and we will talk about it more tomorrow.'

She collected what remained of the food, and the plates and cups, and made her way down the ladder.

'Do you think she doesn't believe us?' asked Lucy. 'I mean about how we got here?'

'I think it's hard to grasp,' said Robert, 'maybe it would be the same for us if the positions were reversed.'

'Maybe she thinks we're on the run from something, and that we'll bring trouble,' suggested Vicky.

'I don't think so,' said Lucy. 'I mean, if she wanted to, she could just tell someone, her uncle or whoever, and just turn us over to them, couldn't she? I think she wants to believe us, but she just doesn't know how.'

'Lucy's right,' said Robert.

Secretly, Lucy smiled to herself. Before, Robert hardly ever spoke directly to her; this was now the second time he had said something to her that sounded like praise.

For a time, they talked on, by the light of the candle, about Anna and her situation, and about their own; they could understand why Anna thought it might be safer for them to move to a bigger place, one where people didn't notice strangers, but they agreed that staying in Alnmouth was still their best chance of finding a way of getting back.

Finally, Robert checked his phone torch, just to reassure them that they could still get some light if they needed it, and then he blew out the candle and they settled into the darkness trying to fall asleep.

The peacefulness was disturbed, maybe an hour later, by a sound of shouting outside. Waking up, Vicky immediately began to panic, thinking someone was breaking in to come upstairs and get them, but at Robert's bidding she quickly calmed down, and she and Lucy comforted each other as they waited.

The noise continued, but it did not get nearer. There was some shouting, some jeering, some raucous laughter.

'It's out on the street,' said Robert. 'Sounds like some kind of squabble. It's not anything to do with us.'

The disturbance lasted for ten minutes or so, and then, gradually, it quietened down, and all was still again.

'It'll be all right now,' said Robert, switching the phone torch on for a minute. 'Let's try to get back to sleep.'

7

Anna came the next morning, bringing, as usual some bread, and a little ham, and the drink she called small beer. The first thing they noticed, however, as her head appeared through the loft hatch, was that the left side of her face, from her eye down over her cheekbone, was covered by a dark ugly bruise.

'You poor thing!' called Lucy.

'What happened? Have you had a fall?'

Anna nodded her head and it seemed that she was about to confirm this, when suddenly, losing control, her face crumpled, and she began to cry.

'Sit down,' said Lucy. She lowered Anna onto a corn sack, and sat beside her, with her arm round her shoulder. Robert and Vicky stood by, awkwardly, catching each other's eye, and exchanging a helpless shrug.

'I'm so afraid of him,' Anna muttered as her sobbing grew less.

Robert kneeled in front of her. 'Abel Slattery. Do you mean him?'

Anna nodded. From close to, Robert could see that her eye was blood-shot around the rim. 'Did he hit you?'

She nodded again. 'It isn't the first time,' she said, now beginning to gain control of her voice. 'Especially when he is drunk, though not usually where people will see the bruises. He hits me with the flat of his hand, sometimes with his fist. Pushes me across the room so that I trip over things. Sometimes he threatens me with other things too, which I daren't even think of.'

She sat for a while longer, and then, seeming to grow embarrassed at the attention of her three guests, stood, and began to arrange the food she had brought for them to eat.

'Did you hear the disturbance on the street outside last night?' she asked, as they ate.

'Yes,' said Robert. 'It sounded like a quarrel or a fight.'

Anna nodded. 'It happens often enough. When the crew of a ship stay in port. They get drunk and argue with themselves or with local men. They think of it as sport. Sometimes, a man gets badly hurt, even killed, but usually it just calms down after a time, and they go back to their drinking. Yesterday it was a ship from Leith that came in. It's often worse with the Scottish boats because of the past troubles.'

'What are the troubles?' asked Robert.

'They tell tales of raids by the Scots. A long time ago. I don't know how long. Setting fire to the village, pillaging anything valuable, that sort of thing.'

'Does it happen now?' asked Vicky, with a note of caution in her voice.

'Not in that way. But old rivalries are still there, in people's minds.'

'Was that how you got your bruise, last night?' asked Vicky.

'No,' said Anna, almost laughing that Vicky should think of her being in a street fight. 'No, it was later, when they had all gone. He made me work at the inn last night. I told you, he sometimes does that when it's busy, or when Dolly doesn't turn in. Taking pots to the tables, bringing them back, washing them. Afterwards, when I was still cleaning, he took hold of me roughly by the arm and tried to make me kiss him. I could smell his breath in my face, all beer and brandy, and I pushed him away, and it was then he walloped me.'

'He must be a monster!' said Lucy.

'It's not usually so bad,' Anna replied. 'It's the fear of it happening as much as anything else.'

'Even so.'

'The other thing - something he said earlier - someone told him I'd been seen in the village with strangers.'

'Us, obviously.'

'He said he was going to speak to me about it, but then he got drunk. He didn't say anything this morning. He was just skulking. I had to wait for him to go down to the harbour before I could come up here, though.'

'Maybe we should go,' said Lucy, looking from Vicky to Robert. 'We can't bring Anna any more trouble.'

'Isn't there anything we can do to help?' asked Robert.

Anna shrugged. 'I don't see how you can. But you don't need to worry today. He's going down to Sunderland with a cargo. He'll be away three or four days.'

'We'll have to talk about a plan.'

'Wouldn't it be good,' suggested Vicky, after Anna had gone, 'if we ever find our way back to our own time, if we could take Anna back with us? ... What?' she added, at the odd looks coming her way from the others.

8

In the evening, when Anna returned, she was able to stay longer than previously. The weather had become milder after the previous day's snow, but it was still cold in the granary, especially during the night. She had managed to find a few more sacks and though some of them had a rather stale smell, they were welcome in the effort to stay warm. During the day, Vicky had been doing her best to lure the cat, with purring noises and clicks of her fingers, and had managed to make it sit on her lap, though when Anna came it immediately jumped down from Vicky, returning to the one it saw as its true mistress.

'Who is that boy you mentioned?' asked Lucy. 'The one who we saw at the beach, and whose clothes you got for Robert?'

'Matty?'

'Yes. Is he really your cousin?'

'No. He is Abel Slattery's nephew, though, so that's how I have to call him. He hates Abel as much as I do. It's the only thing we have in common!'

'Did you ever hear of the Battle of Trafalgar?' said Robert, suddenly. The others turned to him, puzzled, and saw that the question was directed at Anna.

'I think so,' she replied. 'The mariners talk about it.

Was it a sea battle?'

'Yes. Against the French.'

'Then it was probably that, though I wasn't sure about the name.'

'So, when was it? I mean, when was it they were talking about it?'

Anna thought about this for a few moments. 'A few months ago, it must have been, maybe a year,' she said, at last.

'So, if it was about a year ago, it must now be 1806.'

'What's this all about, Robert?' asked Vicky. 'Have we not got enough to think about without worrying about famous sea battles?'

'No, the thing is,' Robert began to explain, 'The Battle of Trafalgar took place in 1805. I know that from school.

And if it was a year ago it must now be 1806.'

'Yes, you said that already.'

'It is,' confirmed Anna. 'Anno Domini, one thousand eight hundred and six. That's what they say in church.'

'And I remember dad telling me that when the river changed its course at Alnmouth, because of a storm like the one we were in, it was 1806. Christmas day, 1806, actually.'

'So?'

'Well, it's now December 1806. How many days is it until Christmas Day, Anna?'

'It's tomorrow fortnight,' she replied.

'Can't you see what I'm getting at?' said Robert, urging the others to think it through and work it out. 'Maybe our best chance of getting back - you know back to our own time - is for us hang on here, if we can, until then, and be on the hill again on Christmas Day.'

No-one seemed to have any reply to this. It was Vicky, at last, who spoke. 'Woden's Hill!' she said. 'I always thought it sounded a bit spooky.'

'If you are going to stay here, then,' said Anna, in a practical tone, 'we have to have another plan, then.'

There was no immediate rush of ideas. It was possible, they all agreed, that they could stay in the granary loft with Anna secretly bringing them food, but to keep it up for a whole two weeks brought with it obvious risks.

'I'd better go,' said Anna, finally. 'Abel Slattery isn't here but it's better if people see me. I don't want to be away too long in case someone asks for me and begins to suspect something.'

After she had gone, the others continued to discuss their situation. They talked about the possibility of going to Alnwick, and getting lodgings for a few days there, but that had its problems too. They had no money to pay for lodgings or food. And even if they could get hold of some money, there was the chance that as children journeying alone, they would be picked out as vagrants, and there was no telling what that might lead to.

As far as staying in Alnmouth was concerned, there was nothing they could do without Anna's involvement, and they all agreed that her life seemed hard enough already without any additional troubles being heaped on her by them.

9

It was Anna, however, who came up with a possible plan, the following morning.

'It will mean bringing Matty into it,' she said, with a tone that hinted at her own misgivings about this. 'He isn't the most trustworthy of people sometimes, but if we can get him to agree to it, it might just be the way of working something out.'

They waited for her to explain.

'He lives with his grandmother – at least I think that's what she is – in a cottage over at Hewgh Field.'

'Hewgh Field? Where's that?'

'Just outside the village, at the top end. It's out of the way.'

'So how does that fit in?'

'Well, Matty sometimes helps out, unloading boats at the jetty, sometimes going out with the fishing cobles. He gets a few pennies that way and usually a few clips round the ear too, but the thing is, if we could persuade him to take Robert along with him, then it wouldn't seem so strange if Robert was seen about in the village. If he was with Matty, people would just think there was some explanation. That's the first bit.'

'I wouldn't mind that,' said Robert. 'Better than being cooped up here all day long.'

'The next bit would be to persuade Matty, or rather, his grandmother, to let Robert and maybe one of you girls stay at the cottage. I don't think it would be big enough for all of you.'

'What about the other one?' asked Lucy.

'Well, you remember I mentioned Dolly?'

'The girl who helps in the tavern?'

'Yes, well, she helps when she's not ailing with something. The thing is, she's missed three days together this week, and my plan is that one of you can stand in for her and stay here in the village with me.'

'What would we have to do?'

'It's not hard. I can show you. It's mainly washing the ale pots and cleaning up. Not very nice, but not too difficult.'

'I don't mind doing that,' said Vicky, looking to Robert for his approval. 'Unless Lucy wants to...'

'No, you do it,' said Lucy. 'I'm not sure I'd like it.'

'But what about when HE gets back?' asked Vicky, remembering the story of Anna's black eye.

'He won't bother you. It's only for a few days. I'll tell him something. If you are standing in for Dolly, he won't be curious.'

They looked one to the other and back again, thinking it through, as if sharing the thought that it was all a bit shaky, but in the end they all nodded their agreement.

'I'll go and find Matty this morning,' said Anna. 'I'll think up some sort of story. He won't ask too many questions. I'll find a bribe for him. He's usually open to a bribe.'

'What about my phone?' suggested Robert. 'You know,' he added, for Anna's benefit, 'the thing that makes light. We could show him that and say, you know,

if he keeps to the plan, I'll give to him?'

'Has it still got any battery?' asked Lucy.

'Enough, I think. Enough for a little demonstration, anyway.'

It was in the middle of the afternoon that the door of the granary below was heard opening, followed by steps on the staircase. Then, at the hatch, Anna appeared, a certain look on her face, followed by the head and face, then the body of the boy who had started the laughing at the ferry, Matty.

He had what seemed a rather silly look on his face, as if he had been brought there for some reward or advantage which he was determined to take advantage of.

'This is Robert,' said Anna. ' And Vicky and Lucy.'

'And where is this magic light thing, then?' was Matty's response, evidently more interested in his own reward than the people concerned.

'We'll show you that, in good time,' said Anna, 'but first, you have to agree to things.'

'What things?' said Matty, a little vacantly.

'First that you take Robert down to the harbour with you, to help him find work. Secondly, that you take Robert and Lucy to your grandma's house, to stay there for a few days. And thirdly...'

'I thought there'd be a thirdly.'

'And thirdly that you keep all this a matter of total secrecy. Do you understand what total secrecy is, Matty?'

'He shrugged. 'Course I do. I'm not stupid, you know.'

'Agreed?'

'Right.' Matty nodded, though not in a way that would inspire anyone with great confidence.

'And then I get the light thing, do I?'

'Yes.'

'How do I know it's not just a trick?'

'I'll show him, shall I?' said Robert, producing his phone from the inside of his jerkin, and switching it on.

Matty watched, waiting, a sly sceptical look on his face.

'I can't see anything,' he said, after a few moments.

'It's warming up. It takes a minute.'

'How much battery have you got?' asked Vicky.

'40%.'

'Should be all right.'

Robert tapped the screen and the narrow cone of blueish light appeared, creating a circle of light on the wall where he was pointing it.

'See!' said Anna, for Matty's benefit. 'Magic light.'

'And I get that, do I? If I help you.'

'And keep it secret.'

'For keeps?'

Robert nodded, then switched the phone off and replaced it inside his jerkin. 'Yes. When we've finished.'

'Remember that,' said Anna. 'When we're finished.'

10

To begin with, Anna instructed Matty to take Robert down to the harbour. They left the granary and made their way back along the alleyway Anna had used when bringing them here a few days before. A sharp wind was blowing up from below, but Robert didn't mind. After being cooped up in the loft for so long, it felt good to be out in the fresh air, cold as it was.

They passed a few people on the way, including two men who nodded to Matty in a casual way of knowing him, but no-one seemed to take exception to Robert as a stranger. It was as Anna had predicted – being alongside Matty seemed to reassure them that he had some acceptable reason for being there, and beyond that they didn't question it.

Now that he wasn't in an immediate hurry, as they had been the other day, Robert was able to take in more of the scene as they approached the estuary and the shore. To begin with, the estuary seemed fuller and wider than he ever remembered it from holidays, even when he had seen it at the highest point of the tide. It was very obvious, too, that there were a lot more boats, and not just rowing boats and small fishing craft, but fully rigged sailing ships with masts and sails. The larger, sea-going vessels were at anchor, or moored in the middle of the flow; others were tied to the sides of a jetty that stretched out into the water for thirty metres, or so. Further upstream, another jetty served a similar purpose.

All along the frontage, business of one kind or another, was going on, and there was a noisy atmosphere of bartering and chatter, against the background noise of weather vanes at the top of masts, clinking in the wind.

A woman, in a bright dress of green and purple and a feathered hat, was waving to try to attract the attention of the sailors of a tender coming towards the jetty from a two masted brigantine anchored out in the estuary.

'That's Lily Appleby,' said Matty. 'Folk say she's no better than she should be, her and her sisters.'

'Watch out, youngster. What mischief are you up to?'

'Looking for jobs. Me and my pal.'

'Oh aye! Is he anywhere near as lazy as you.'

'He's a good'un,' said Matty. 'You try him and see.'

The man looked at them, pushed his cap back, scratched his head, and then said, 'See them baskets on the far jetty? Fetch them down this way to the cart. And mind you spill nothing.'

There was a pile of twelve baskets. Matty hoisted one up onto his shoulder, but immediately dropped it down again.

'It's alive!' he shouted.

Robert peeked inside. The basket was full of crabs, clambering over one another in an attempt to escape.

'Put one box on the other,' said Robert. 'Then you take one end, I'll do the other.'

'Right,' said Matty, somewhat put out that Robert had come up with the way to do it.

In this way, they moved the baskets to the cart at the end of the harbour, where the man was waiting, smoking a pipe, and chatting to another man. He gave them a farthing each.

'Is that all?' Matty complained.

'Never mind *is that all*, let me get hold of you, I'll show you what's all.'

Matty just managed to step out of the way of a swipe aimed at his ear.

'Come on,' he said to Robert. 'Always was a tight one, him. We'll find someone else.'

After Robert left with Matty, Anna took Vicky next door to the inn. They entered by a door at the back, and went up a staircase to a landing above, and then to another landing above that. Finally, they reached an attic room right at the top of the house. Here, Anna opened a door to a room with a bed and small roof window looking out over the street below.

'This is where I sleep,' said Anna. 'You can share with me. You'll feel safer if we're together.'

Vicky nodded her head in agreement. 'What are all the other rooms?'

'Abel Slattery has two rooms. A sitting room and his bed chamber. The rest are for lodgers. Sailors mainly. But they just come and go. Usually just one night.'

Downstairs, a burly man in a leather apron was unloading stuff from the dray down into the cellar.

'Will!' called Anna, to attract his attention. 'This is Vicky. She's going to help out whilst Dolly is ailing.'

The man nodded and turned back to his work.

'Will is the cellarman and tap man. It'll be him you see most, and as you can probably tell, he's a man of few words. Abel Slattery does his drinking in the other taverns in the town, mostly. As you may have noticed, there are plenty of them. It's only when he gets back here late on and drunk that he gets nasty. But he wouldn't do anything while Will is still around.'

'I'm glad!'

'I'll show you the scullery. There isn't much to do now, but this is where the pots come to be washed, and then hung up on the pegs. If you do want to do something whilst I take Lucy to see Matty's Granny, you could sweep up, and then take a duster round the sitting room on the first floor up. I've already seen to Abel Slattery's chamber, so there's nothing to be done there before he gets back.'

'Right,' said Vicky. 'Show me where everything is and I'll get on with it.'

'First, we'll just walk down the main street together, arm-in-arm as if we know each other well. Let people have a glimpse of you with me. We can get some things to take with Lucy, too.'

The street outside was busy, with people coming and going into shops, pushing carts, and other business.

They stopped to buy some bread at a baker's stall, some tea, some whiting which had just been landed. At the bottom of the street, on the piece of land which they'd called the ferry, there were a few stalls like a small market. A man with a cow was allowing it to graze where there was a patch of grass amidst the sandy scrub. Opposite, Vicky could see Woden's Hill, looking larger than she remembered it, and the ruins of the church walls stood out clearly on the summit. As they stood there, a two masted sloop appeared on the seaward side, and Vicky remembered that the channel of the river was on the far side of the hill.

'That was fine,' said Anna when they returned. 'No-one turned a hair. Now, if you'll be all right here on your own for an hour, I'll take Lucy over to Matty's Granny's cottage.'

It was a twenty-minute walk. From the edge of the village, a winding track led uphill, branching off at one point with a path which climbed to a high summit, which Anna called Mount Pleasant, and which, she said, was also the village 'common'. Further on, they came to a small cottage lying in the crook of a wall beneath a group of trees, now in their winter bareness. A line at the side carried some sheets flapping in the wind, and a thin trail of smoke rose from the chimney, before being dispersed through the air. As Anna and Lucy approached, a small figure, evidently Matty's Granny, was carrying a bucket towards the side door. Anna called and the old woman turned, screwing up her eyes, which looked watery with the cold and the wind, to see who was there.

After a moment, she seemed to recognise Anna, and she beckoned them into the house. There was slight smell of damp and smoke, but it had a homely feel. Pointing for them to sit, she added some coals to a small fire in the hearth, all the time talking to herself, and mumbling under her breath. She walked with a stoop and her face was lined with deep shadowy wrinkles, but her pale blue eyes seemed to have a gentle kindly look.

'This is Lucy,' said Anna.

'Who?'

'Lucy,' Anna repeated, raising her voice. Then, turning to Lucy, 'She's a little hard of hearing,' she added. 'Lucy. She is my cousin from Alnwick.'

'Yes. Alnwick,' repeated the old woman, as if that, at least, had some meaning for her.

'She is with her brother. He is called Robert.'

The old lady peered, screwing her face up, somewhere between borderline understanding and complete incomprehension.

'He is with Matty,' Anna continued.

At the mention of Matty, the old lady responded immediately with a tut-tut-tut noise that went on for some time like a chicken clucking its disapproval. 'They need some lodgings while they are in Alnmouth, just for a few days.'

'Who?'

'Lucy...' she persisted, and then, after a pause, 'And Robert.'

The old lady now turned her attention to Lucy, taking both of her hands into her own and rubbing and squeezing them as if she was trying to keep Lucy warm.

Lucy smiled, and the old lady leaned back, fanning her fingers over her mouth and cheeks, almost as if studying her.

'I think she likes you,' said Anna.

'And I like her,' said Lucy, offering her hands which the old lady took.

Patiently, and slowly, Anna explained and repeated the proposed arrangement until she was confident that it had been understood.

'Do you want to come back with me, Lucy, and then come back later when Robert's with you?'

'No, I'll stay here,' Lucy replied. 'I'll help her a little, get to know her.'

'Yes, all right. That's a good idea. Then, Matty can bring Robert over later.'

Robert and Matty returned to the granary later in the afternoon, having made the grand sum of threepence from their labours. Matty claimed he should have the larger share as he had been in charge of getting jobs; Robert said he did not particularly mind, but Anna insisted that they should share it equally. 'You don't know when it might be useful to have some money in your pocket, Robert,' she said.

'Have you got anything for us to eat, then?' asked Matty, looking for some kind of compensation.

Anna went back to the tavern and brought a portion of a veal pie which Matty stuffed down.

'Will you be all right?' said Robert to Vicky, who had come back up with Anna.

She nodded her head quickly, several times, and grinned, as if glad to be embarking on her own adventure.

Finally, Robert and Matty set off back to the cottage, and Anna and Vicky went down to the scullery of the tavern to begin their evening's work.

11

Two days passed. Anna's plan seemed to be working like a charm. Lucy and Granny Matty, as they started to call her, took to each other in a way which might have been predicted from their first meeting. Lucy helped with the chores around the house; Granny complained about Matty with her typical tut-tut-tut, whenever his name came up; and they enjoyed each other's company, often laughing, even when they didn't fully understand what the other was saying.

Vicky took to her work in the tavern with equal enthusiasm. True, as the evenings wore on, it was increasingly raucous and smoky; and the men, as she took them their pots and collected them back again, did not spare their cussing and swearing, but it did not put her off, and she was aware that Anna, and to a lesser extent, Will – though he said nothing – were keeping an eye out for her.

For Robert, putting up with Matty - who was lazy and often less than fully truthful - was a burden, but he stuck to it, and by the end of the week, he had close on a shilling in his pocket, which, he reckoned by a vague calculation, was worth about twenty pounds in modern money. Maybe a bit more, maybe a bit less, but worth having, for sure.

On Sunday, Anna went to church, as was expected, and Vicky said she wanted to go too. The church on Woden's Hill was too dilapidated and dangerous for services these days, its main use now, Anna told them, being as a cemetery, but there was a small chapel in the village, and that's where Anna went to the Sunday morning service. Later, all four of them met, and walked up towards Boulmer, the next village along the coast. On the way, they passed a field where some horses were grazing, two chestnuts, a brown and a grey. 'Look at them!' called Lucy. 'Aren't they lovely!'

'You like horses?' asked Anna.

'I love horses,' she replied. 'At home, I go riding whenever I can. It's my best thing.'

They stood watching for a few minutes and then walked on, into the village. On the way back, they took the lower path, collecting sea-coals from the shore, to contribute to Granny Matty's stock of fuel.

It was a mild day for the time of year. Apart from a cool soft breeze coming from the sea, the air was still, and the quiet was only disturbed by the soft slap of the waves breaking and sending their tongues of foamy surf up the beach. Robert was walking with Anna, Vicky and Lucy were playing by the fringe of the sea, looking for shells as well as coals.

'They seem happy,' said Anna.

'Yes. It's almost as if they really live here. I mean, as if they're beginning to forget the other world we've come from.'

'And what about you?'

'I don't know. When I was younger, I used to make things up in my imagination, fantasy worlds to play in, and as long as I was playing, they seemed to be true, as if they really existed. The last couple of nights, I've lain there wondering if I haven't somehow invented all this.'

'Well, you haven't invented me,' said Anna.

'No,' said Robert.

When they came to the rocks at Seaton Point, Anna indicated they should take the steep path up the slope of the hillside. Robert went first, turning to make sure the others were keeping up. Then came Anna, and behind them, Vicky and Lucy. At the top, another path led by a back way to the cottage.

'Did you see that?' said Vicky to Lucy, with a giggle.

'What?'

'When they thought we weren't looking. Robert and Anna, coming up from the beach. They were holding hands.'

'I thought he was just helping her up where it was a big step up,' Lucy replied.

'Maybe,' said Vicky, thoughtfully. 'It could be that they are falling in love, though.'

They thought about this for a moment, and then, both together, allowed themselves a burst of quiet giggling.

And so, the two days passed.

On the third day, Abel Slattery returned.

12

And that was also the day when Robert had a fight with Matty. They were down on the quay, carrying sacks along to the end of the jetty, where they were to be loaded onto a boat due to leave for Newcastle later in the morning. It was a cold morning, colder than most recent days, but it was heavy work, and by the time they had moved half the load, Robert was hot.

'I'm sweating cobs,' he announced. He took off his jerkin, and placed it out of the way, behind a post near the wall.

'Come on, you lads!' called the man who had set them on. 'No slacking or there'll be no pay!'

Robert heaved another sack onto his aching shoulder. Complaining in a low mumble of being treated like a slave, Matty, too, lifted another sack, and together they trundled along the jetty, and then back for another trip.

Once again Robert hoisted a sack onto his shoulder. Matty followed suit, but then, having cast his eye around, and seeing that the master was somewhere out of sight, he let it drop to the ground again. 'Look,' he said, 'I'm all in – I'm just going to have a quick blow.'

A 'blow', as Robert had learned was Matty's way of saying he was going to sneak away somewhere to have a rest, and the description of 'quick' was not always accurate. 'Tell him I needed a *you-know-what* if he comes back. I'll do the same for you.'

Realising it was better not to argue, Robert set out with his load along the jetty.

'What's up with your pal, then?' asked the man loading the sacks onto the boat.

'He's just gone for a *what's-it*,' Robert replied.

'No, he hasn't,' said the man, nodding towards the shore, 'he's having a sit-down over there.'

Looking back, Robert saw that Matty was sitting by the post where he had left his jerkin. Not only that, but also that Matty had his jerkin on his lap and was going through the pockets.

Incensed, he started off back at a pace which quickly broke into a run.

'Oy!' he shouted out. 'Get off that. Put it down!'

He assumed that Matty was intending to steal the few coins he had in one of the pockets, but as he drew close, it dawned on him that what Matty was really looking for was the phone.

'Get off that!' he said, standing over Matty.

He grabbed a corner of the jerkin, and pulled, but Matty gripped onto it with both hands, refusing to let go. 'Give it me!' he replied. 'It's mine, anyway, you gave it me. It was a promise.'

'Only when everything's done.'

'I don't know what you mean by everything. I've done everything she said. I'm not waiting anymore.'

'Yes, you are,' said Robert, and with a sudden sharp tug, he pulled the jerkin out of Matty's hands. Matty let out a stream of foul names aimed at Robert, and then, as if he'd roused his own anger to fever-pitch, he got up, and hurled himself at Robert, so that the sudden force made Robert stagger backwards. He tried to unloose himself from the clasp, but Matty's greater weight and bulk gave him the advantage. The struggle lasted for nearly half a minute, and then two of the men who had gathered, and who were laughing at the clumsy contest, pulled them roughly apart.

Robert was breathless, even shaking a little, and he felt that tears were not a long way behind his eyes. But he was glad the men had pulled them apart because he realised that - much as Matty might be a poor physical specimen overall - there was no way that Robert could actually match him, strength for strength, in a fight.

Matty however looked as if his rage was still up. As soon as the man let go of his shoulders, he made another bolt for Robert, who was quick enough to dodge, and side-step away. But this was not the end of it. Matty turned and began another charge. This time, Robert had no room to dodge, so he turned and ran, and with nowhere else to go, found himself running onto the further jetty. Matty, too, was now out of breath, but he kept coming on, with his head lowered as if he was going to charge Robert like a bull. Robert now simply stood still. He was only feet away from the end of the jetty.

'All right,' he said. 'All right. Enough.'

'Give me the thing.'

'You know what the agreement is.'

'Give it me.'

'No.'

At this, Matty lurched forward again. In response Robert rose onto his tip toes, and at the very last moment, just as Matty was about make a grab for him, he made a sudden swerve, and the momentum of Matty's lunge took him to the edge of the jetty, where with one foot poised on the edge, he tried, for two or three seconds, to maintain his balance, and then dropped, with a gasp into the water. In panic, he thrashed about and crashed about in the water, shouting out that he was drowning, but in fact the water was no more than a couple of feet deep, and after a while he was standing to his full height, with the water just up to his knees.

But the coldness of the water had taken the last of the fight out of him, and he waded to the edge, disappearing towards the village, and no doubt from there to his granny's cottage.

Robert made his way back to the first jetty, ready to continue work, but by now the rest of the sacks had gone, and had already been loaded onto the boat, which was now preparing to get under sail. He looked towards the gaffer who had set them on, but it was clear from the sour expression on his face, that any payment from him had been forfeited.

Disconsolately, he wandered back to the bottom of the village. He knew he would have to tell Anna what had happened, and hope that she would be able to do something to rescue the situation with Matty, but apart from meeting at the granary, or at Matty's granny's cottage, by arrangement, he did not know how to get into contact with her. Luckily, he spotted Vicky, who had been sent down to buy something from one of the market stalls.

'Tell Anna I've had a bit of a scrape with Matty. Ask her if she can meet me at the granary.'

'It's busy there today,' said Vicky. 'They're moving a lot of stuff down to the harbour and fetching some new stuff in. Lots of people about. But I'll tell her and see what she says. Wander past in about ten minutes.'

Robert was fairly sure that he could move about the town now without attracting any undue attention or unwanted curiosity, but even so, he made his way by the narrow roundabout alleys that he was now becoming familiar with, sometimes noting places, angles of walls, turns, perspectives that were an earlier version of the Alnmouth he knew from his holidays with Vicky and their mum and dad.

When he arrived, by the back way, at the inn, he waited in the shadow of the passageway, and a few moments later Anna herself came out.

'What's happened?' she asked.

He gave her a quick account of the morning's incidents, leading up to Matty's dousing in the cold water of the harbour.

'Sounds as if he deserved it!' she said, barely concealing a grin. 'I'd better go along there and smooth things over. Don't worry. I could tell one or two tales on him that would get him more than he bargained for from Abel Slattery.'

They had walked together back down the alley and were about to emerge on the quayside near the jetty where the incident had taken place, when Anna stopped suddenly. 'Talk of the Devil!' she said.

'What?' said Robert, puzzled.

Anna gestured across the estuary to where a three masted schooner was just appearing, coming into the haven from behind Woden's Hill.

'That's his ship,' she replied, in a hushed voice. 'Abel Slattery is back.'

13

∽

Vicky was washing the last of the pots from the afternoon drinking, when a loud bang, just behind her, made her jump nearly out of her skin.

'Who are you to be in here, wench!' came a low throaty gravelly voice. The voice belonged to Abel Slattery, and the loud bang was that of his clenched fist striking the table just behind her in a fierce blow.

Turning, and lifting the dishcloth to her chin in fear, Vicky set eyes for the first time on the owner of the voice and the fist.

'If it please you, sir...' she mumbled in a thin and tremulous voice. It was a phrase she remembered reading in a book somewhere, and she hoped it would do, though what she was going to say after it, she had no idea.

'If what please me?' he returned, taking a step closer. 'If what please me, come on, slip, speak up!'

At this moment, much to Vicky's relief, Anna, having heard the disturbance, appeared at the door to the scullery. 'She's called Vicky,' she said firmly, ' and she's doing Dolly's work for her, and you should be grateful to her and to me for it.'

'Grateful to you, wench!' he said in a tone of ridicule. The insults which he came out with next - all aimed at Anna - were garbled, and there were some words which Vicky had not heard before, but the intention was clear enough.

'You're drunk,' Anna said, plainly, not backing down.

It seemed to Vicky that this was probably true. The man was wearing a sailor's greatcoat, fully unbuttoned, with a grubby red scarf tied loosely about his neck and an equally grubby yellow waistcoat beneath. On his head was a three-corner hat, slightly askew, with tufts of hair, black streaked with grey, hanging onto his brow and temples and pushed back behind his ears. His face was red and his eyes slightly blood-shot. He could, thought Vicky, be anywhere between thirty and fifty, and was certainly not a pleasant sight.

Seeing that Anna was determined not to be threatened by him in this instance, he grinned, and made a throaty laugh, which seemed to say, don't think you won the game yet, there's plenty still to play for. Then, his body seemed to collapse slightly inwards, a bit like a balloon that has lost some of its air, and he turned, stumbling slightly against the table, and walked past her in the direction of the stairs. There, he turned, and, holding onto the balustrade, said, 'If Erskine comes here tonight, tell him I'll call on him tomorrow, nice and bright and early.'

For a while after his departure, the two girls stood in silence. Anna, who had seemed to remain calm, now took measured deep breaths, as if to control a storm that was brewing within.

'It's all right,' she said at last, in a quiet reassuring voice. 'Now that he's seen you, that's good, he probably won't notice you again.'

'I hope he doesn't. What a brute.'

'His boat came in on the tide, just past noon. He will have been drinking since then. That's when he's at his worst.'

'Who is Erskine that he mentioned?'

'Thomas Erskine. He's the Prevention Officer?'

'What's that mean?'

'He's the man who's supposed to make a record of all the cargos that come in and go out from Alnmouth. He probably should have reported to him earlier.'

'But why 'prevention'? What is he supposed to be preventing?'

'Smuggling,' said Anna.

Robert had agreed to let Matty have the phone in his hands and to play with it for few minutes. The battery was now down to 18%, and he knew that it would waste quickly with the torch switched on, but that was the deal that Anna had negotiated, earlier in the afternoon. Once he had dried himself off and put fresh clothes on, it was only his hurt pride that needed to be mended.

'I was just lucky,' Robert said, trying to help this along. 'You're much stronger than me. In a proper fist fight you'd win any day. All I could do was run.'

'Like a coward,' suggested Matty.

'Yes. Just like a coward,' Robert agreed, and he saw Anna winking at him from across the room.

In the end, Anna had not needed to bring out the threats of what she could tell Abel Slattery about things Matty had got up to, but the mere mention of his name, as when she mentioned that his ship had come back into port, seemed enough to set Matty on edge.

Whilst Robert was doing his best to appease Matty, Anna had taken Lucy aside. 'The other day, you were saying that you liked horses, you know, when you were back at home.'

'Yes. I do. Very much.'

'Then, there's something you can help me with, if you will.'

'What is it? To do with horses?'

'Abel Slattery has a horse which he keeps at the farm stables. Now that he is back, he will want it made ready for riding. Usually, he sends me on this errand, but it's better if I stay to keep an eye on Vicky. Will you go for me?'

'Yes,' said Lucy, enthusiastically. 'But which farm is it?'

'It's not far from here. If you follow the path a little further, you will come to it directly. Tom is the name of the stableman. He's quite nice.'

'Yes, I'd love to.'

'I thought you would. And it'll give you something to do. You must be bored, stuck here all day with Granny Matty.'

'It's not so bad. We've become quite good friends.'

'Yes, I'd noticed. She likes you being here. She'll miss you.'

'I'll miss her. If we ever get away, that is. I mean, we all think it will happen, but it's only because Robert had the idea about Christmas Day and the storm. I sometimes think that here and now is where I really live, and that it's the other that's not really real.'

'We'll see if Robert is right.'

'I mean, he's probably right about the storm and the river, because that really happened, but about us getting back, well it's just a guess. We haven't a clue really.'

14

On the evening of his return, Abel Slattery made no further appearances in the scullery of the inn, nor in its public bar or its parlour. Anna and Vicky were kept busy, because a number of the men drinking in the evening had arrived in the port that day and were lodging at the inn during their stay. Peggy, a large jolly woman, always in a clean apron and mop cap, came in when it was required to cook food for them in the kitchen, which added to the stacks of washing up that came back for Vicky to deal with. Anna took round the pots when Will had filled them and brought the plates and empties back into the scullery.

'Let me have a go,' said Vicky. 'We'll swap for a bit.'

'Are you sure you want to? They can be very rough tongued, you know.'

'I don't mind. I can hear it from here anyway.'

So, Anna had a word with Will, and Vicky dried her hands and went into the parlour, trying to adopt a suitably pert expression, as of one who was confident about what she was doing.

There was a big fire in the grate, and you could feel the heat of it on your face as you walked past. The pipe smoke was almost like a fog in the room, and the chatter was rowdy, but it was cheerful and hearty, and apart from a little good-natured banter about the cheeky new barmaid, there was nothing to make Vicky feel upset. In fact, she quite enjoyed it. It was better than washing up.

'Are you all right?' asked Anna, now with her own sleeves rolled up.

'Yes. It's fun.'

'Not what I'd call fun, but you're welcome to it!'

'They're quite jolly, really. There's just one man who came in a while ago, sitting on his own just by the door looking quite solemn.'

Anna dried her hands and went to look.

'That's him,' she said on her return. 'Thomas Erskine. The Prevention man. I passed Abel's message on to him. He's gone now.'

'Is Abel Slattery really smuggling things?'

'Don't let anyone hear you saying that. Especially not himself. There are some things it's better not to know.'

When he did appear, the following morning, Abel Slattery sat in the parlour, hunched over his plate, a dark and morose look on his face. He looked up, sourly, when Vicky took him the coffee he had demanded, but he said nothing. He seemed to have accepted that she was there and was simply doing a job. When he had finished eating, he pulled on his greatcoat and hat, and set off from the inn, on his way, they presumed, to see the Prevention man.

After she had helped Granny Matty to set the fire and to peg out some linen that they had washed and wrung out together, Lucy put on her cloak, and set out towards the farm. Robert and Matty, now pals again, it seemed, had been discussing plans of some sort, and had left for the port as usual after their breakfast. Too excited at the prospect of her errand to bother about anything else, Lucy had not even tried to listen to their conversation.

The path to the farm, along the edge of a field, had become muddy under foot in places, but Lucy managed to pick her way without getting her shoes too wet or mucky. She found herself going between two outbuildings onto a cobbled yard, strewn with bits of loose straw. Half a dozen chickens were pecking busily, their heads bobbing up and down in quick taps, and a strong smell of farm manure wafted out from the shed where, as she could now see, cows were stalled.

'How do, then, missy?' came a voice, and a man appeared pushing a wheelbarrow around the corner of the barn.

'I've come with a message,' Lucy said, by way of explanation.

'Oh, yes, and how's that then?'

'It's from Mr Slattery.'

'Oh yes,' said the man, pushing his hat back on his brow. 'He's back, then, is he?'

Lucy sensed from his tone that Abel Slattery's return was not something the man particularly, welcomed.

'Are you Tom?' she asked.

The man grinned. 'Tom. That's me. And who's asking?'

'I'm Lucy,' she said.

'Lucy, eh? I don't suppose you're any good at milking are you, Lucy?'

'I'm afraid not.'

'More's the pity. I could have done with some help there this morning.'

'I'll have a go, if you like.'

The man's grin turned into a smile. 'Perhaps you'd best tell me what your message is first, Lucy. About Gimlet I'll wager.'

'Is Gimlet the name of Mr Slattery's horse?'

'It is.'

'Then yes. Anna asked me to tell you that he will be wanting his horse made ready.'

Tom nodded. 'And how is Anna, then?'

'Very well, thank you very much,' said Lucy, trying to express herself in a polite way, and thinking that she could hardly say, *very well, apart from the occasional black eye, that is.*

'We worry about her sometimes,' said Tom. 'Me and Jessie – Jessie being my wife, like – we do. We worry about her being in that place with him. He's not known for his smooth manners, like, or his kindness.'

'Yes, I've heard.'

Tom nodded slowly but said nothing more. 'Well,' he said at last, 'you've delivered your message Lucy, and you can say that Gimlet will be ready when he wants her.'

'Is she's a filly, then? Or a mare?'

'Right first time. A filly. Know horses, do you, Lucy?'

'Just a bit. May I see her before I go back?'

'Come on, then, I don't see any harm in that.'

He pushed the barrow to one side, let go of the handles, and wiped his hands with a rag he pulled from his pocket. Then he led the way to another part of the farm, and into a brick building with stalls along one side, and with feeding troughs and water buckets.

'Mainly farm horses we keep ourselves. Workers.'

'They're lovely,' said Lucy, stopping to stroke the head of each of the long-maned horses as she passed.

Gimlet was in the last stall.

'There she is,' said Tom.

'Hello Gimlet,' said Lucy, gently tapping its nose and stroking its head. The horse gave out a low whinny, making Lucy laugh.

'Want to walk her round?' asked Tom. She nodded a definite yes.

'I don't ride myself,' said Tom, as he assembled the tackle and fitted the reins. 'As I say, it's just the work horses for me, but he stables Gimlet here when he's not wanting her.'

They walked outside into the yard, drawing Gimlet, willingly, along on the reins. Her colouring was a rich dark brown and she was about fourteen hands high. There was a thick white stripe down her nose and her front hooves had white cuffs.

'She's gorgeous,' said Lucy. 'She reminds me of Joanie. That's one of the horses I ride at home.'

'Oh, you ride, then, do you, young Lucy?'

'Yes, whenever I can.'

'You just wait here, then.'

On a sudden whim, Tom went back into the stable and came back with the saddle and girth, stirrups, and a saddle cloth. These, he fastened into place, tightening the straps, and Gimlet, anticipating a ride, pawed the ground with one hoof.

Tom was going to help Lucy get up into the saddle but there was no need. She quickly put her foot in the stirrup and confidently hoisted herself up, settling in the saddle despite the awkwardness of her skirts.

'No side-saddle for you then, missy!' he said.

At first, he led her along through the yard and onto the field, but once there, seeing how comfortable she was, he let her take the reins, and Lucy soon had the horse at a trot and then a canter.

'That was brilliant!' she said, at last swinging down off the horse to the ground.

'Well, usually when he wants her, he sends a message and I walk her down, but I reckon he should send you and you can ride her over. Save me a journey.'

'Yes, I should like that,' said Lucy.

'Goodbye then, Miss Lucy,' he called as she set off on her journey back.

'Bye, Tom. Thanks. See you again soon, I hope.'

'That's *Merry Joan*,' said Matty, pointing out across the estuary to the ship Robert had seen coming in yesterday, now moored fifty or sixty yards off the shore.

'Abel Slattery's ship?' said Robert.

'Yes. How did you know that?'

'Heard someone say yesterday, after you'd gone.' Robert replied, thinking it best not to mention his conversation with Anna.

It was a slack day down at the dock. Matty and Robert had been hovering about looking for any sign that there was work to be had. There was nothing doing. Sitting now on a low wall overlooking the river, they were idling time away by throwing stones into the water.

'They mustn't have unloaded her yet,' said Matty.

'That's odd.'

'Why?'

'They usually get on with it.'

'What's the cargo?'

Matty shrugged his shoulders. 'Depends. Coal, sometimes. Wood. Usually, a keg or two of brandy to slip past the Prevention man. Might just be ballast if he's not in a hurry.'

'What's that, then? Ballast?'

'Ships need a weight in them. If there's no decent cargo to bring back, they sometimes fill them with rubble and stone, just for the weight. Only they usually dump it before they come in. They get a fine if they drop it in the estuary.'

'Have you been on it, the Merry Joan?'

'Loads of times,' Matty boasted. 'I can show you if you like.'

'How can you do that?' Robert replied, doubtful that the boast meant anything, and also doubtful, if it was true, of the wisdom of taking him up on it.

'Easy,' said Matty. 'Just get a tender from up the shore, and row out. Get close enough to have a scan. Say we're out doing a bit of fishing if anyone asks.'

'What's a tender? A rowing boat?'

'Same as.'

In spite of his doubts, Robert was tempted by the thought of a boat ride out into the river. 'How can you just get one, though?'

'There are plenty. A lot are just used at night, for the lobster pots like. No-one'll notice. I've done it plenty times.'

Again, Robert doubted this casual boast, but he was prepared to see if Matty could back it up.

They walked further up the shore, until they were out of sight of the main part of the port. It was true that there were plenty of small craft pulled up onto the sand and grass of the upper shore, mostly tied up to posts or with chains wrapped around heavy rocks.

'This one,' said Matty suddenly, choosing one of the smaller ones, and beginning to untie it.

'Are you sure this is a good idea?'

'Come on, they'll never know.'

He quickly finished untying the boat. It was flatbottomed and light, which made it quite easy to pull over the sand. Then they pushed it out into the shallow water and stepped inside. Robert sat in the prow, Matty used one of the oars as a pole to push out against the bottom and then sat down and fixed the oars into the rowlocks and began to row.

Once they got away from the shore, there was a stiffer wind, rippling the surface of the water, and the boat began to respond to the current. Matty was sufficiently proficient, however, to use the current to pull them round onto the far side of the Merry Joan, and after five minutes they came alongside in the boat's shadow. It seemed much bigger close to, when they were looking up from the level of the water. She was anchored fore and aft, and just riding slightly with the swell. There appeared to be no-one on board.

'Let's take a look,' said Matty.

'This is enough,' said Robert, once again doubting the wisdom of what they were doing. 'Let's get back.'

But Matty had set his eye on a rope ladder, left hanging over the side, dipping into the water, and he angled the little boat towards it.

'Let's just take a peek,' he said. 'No harm in that.'

Without waiting to hear Robert's opinion on this, he tied up to the ladder, rested the oars in the locks, and pulled himself onto the first rungs. 'I'll nip up and see the coast's clear,' he grinned.

Robert watched him go. The ladder swayed with his weight, but step by step he ascended the dozen or so rungs, spent a short time peeping over the rail, and then climbed over onto the deck.

Robert waited below. A minute. Two minutes. He wondered what he would do, now, if Matty was caught at it, trespassing. Would he be able to cast free and row back? Or would the current be too strong for his inexperienced rowing. He would probably just have to stay here until he, too, was caught. Then, Matty's grinning face appeared over the rail again, beckoning Robert to follow.

Once on the ladder, it seemed to sway much more perilously than it had with Matty on it, and more than once his stomach clenched in panic at the thought that he would lose his grip and fall back into the water, which now looked deep and ominous below him. Then Matty's arm reached down, and his hand gripped Robert's shoulder, helping him over the rail.

'Welcome aboard cap'n,' said Matty, with a grin.

Robert looked around, still fearful that someone would suddenly appear, and not appreciative of Matty's humour. Looking back towards the shore, there was no sign of any activity that might be connected to the Merry Joan, and it was probably the case that, unless someone was looking with a spyglass, they themselves would not be easily visible from the shore.

Matty now beckoned him towards a small cabin door leading into the fo'c'sle. Inside, sprawled over a table, and snoring, with an empty bottle of something beside him, and a candle that was still burning, was an old man with matted hair and a white beard. Another man, younger, but in the same state, lay sprawled along the floor.

'Watchmen,' said Matty, with a smirk. 'Best sober up before Abel gets back, I'd say, or it'll be the other drink they'll be in.'

'Let's get back,' urged Robert.

'What for? There's no danger.'

'Even so. What else is there to see?'

'You wanted to know what the cargo was. Let's take a look.'

He led the way to the rear of the ship, where two hatches were set in the deck, and urged Robert to help him lift one of them by its rings. They struggled for a while, but at last the stiffness of the hinges began to give and, inch by inch, the hatch door came upwards. It pivoted, and then they let it fall backwards onto the deck, with a bang, leaving a space of darkness below.

With an instinctive nervous reaction, Robert looked back towards the fo'c'sle to see if the noise had disturbed those within, but there was nothing. Another moment, nothing.

They peered down into the darkness.

As their eyes adjusted, they began to make out the shape of sacks below.

'Coal,' said Matty.

'Yes, coal. Like you said,' Robert replied. 'Now let's get this hatch back in place and get away.'

'Wait a minute,' said Matty. 'There's something else. A different smell. It's not just coal. Shine the thing down.'

'What thing?'

'The light thing.'

'I haven't brought it with me,' said Robert.

Matty sighed heavily with frustration.

'Let's just go,' said Robert, 'What's the point?'

'Just a minute,' said Matty, and with that he went back to the cabin in the fo'c'sle and came out again with the candle, shielding its flame. Then, leaning over the entrance to the hold, he lowered the candle, and both he and Robert put their heads down and looked. Beyond the bags of coal, row on row, and stack on stack, were barrels.

'Brandy,' said Matty. 'That's what the smell is...'

Before he could say anything else, there was a buffet of air, like a small explosion which threw both of them back onto the deck.

'What was that?' said Robert, recovering from the shock.

'Must be fumes,' said Matty. 'Fumes from the brandy, must have caught the candle flame.'

'Quick, then, let's get the hatch into place.'

This time, Matty did not disagree, and together they lifted the hatch door and dropped it back into place. They looked at each other with a shared sense of mischief.

'If you dropped a lighted rag down there,' Matty said.

'The whole ship would go up.'

'No thanks,' said Robert. 'Not with us on it.'

'Some barrels must have burst. I thought I could smell it.'

'Come on. Let's get out before anything else happens.'

Again, Matty did not disagree, and a few moments later, they were swinging on the rope ladder as they climbed down to the tender. Then, much to Robert's relief, the Merry Joan was growing smaller to the view, as each stroke of the oars increased the distance between them.

15

～

Abel Slattery had been sitting with Thomas Erskine, the Prevention Officer, for a good two hours. They were sitting alone in the parlour, and Abel Slattery had made it more than clear that no-one else was to be permitted entrance to the parlour until their business was concluded.

Jessie, the cook, had been allowed to take two plates of food to them. Vicky, finding it difficult to conceal her nerves, had been sent through by Jessie to fetch the plates when they were done with them. Anna had been called on for a bottle and glasses, and then again, half an hour later, for a second bottle.

What the nature of the business was that was being discussed, no-one, apart from the two men, had any clear idea. Those coming out of the room with dishes, bottles and glasses had agreed, in their shared whisperings, that there was a degree of tension between the men, and that there was probably some kind of negotiation going on where both men were striking a hard deal. It seemed reasonable to deduce that the business was to do with the cargo, still unladen, which Abel Slattery, the Master of the Merry Joan had brought into Alnmouth harbour just the day before.

Jessie seemed to think that she had caught a part of a sentence in which Thomas Erskine was complaining that Abel Slattery had not yet presented his papers, and when Vicky asked what this meant, it was explained to her that the papers which a ship brought with it were the official documents that certified what its cargo was and also certifying that its cargo had been approved as being legal, and that all duties and fees pertaining to it had been paid.

When fetching the plates away, Vicky had heard Abel Slattery say that he was damned if he was going to go back to Berwick, though she did not hear enough to make any more sense of it than its plain meaning, except that the expectation of foul weather was a factor.

'Ah,' said Jessie, 'but you see, Berwick is where all the official papers are stamped. So, he must be making an excuse out of it.'

Anna, taking in the second bottle, caught a part of a sentence, muttered under his breath, asserting that he, Thomas Erskine, was not to be made a fool of, and lingering a little by the door, she had also picked up Abel Slattery's assurance that a little patience on his part would be well rewarded.

What it all boiled down to, it was concluded, was that there was something suspicious about the cargo of the Merry Joan, and that Abel Slattery was sounding Thomas Erskine out on what kind of price would be needed for him to turn a blind eye to it.

'For Thomas Erskine,' Jessie opined, 'is as full of wickedness as Abel Slattery. You couldn't slip a wafer between them.'

At half past seven, the two men got up and left the Sun Inn together and a lighter atmosphere began to prevail. The talk in the public bar now was of the weather, which, it appeared was predicted by those who knew something about it, to be about to take a turn for the worse in time for Christmas. Hearing this, Anna and Vicky caught each other's eye, and a questioning look passed between them.

It was a busy evening, however, and neither of the two had much time to dwell on her own thoughts, as the pots were hurried back and forth, washed, dried, filled at the keg by Will and taken back again to the tables. The general atmosphere was mirthful and loud. The more ale and spirits the company drank, the jollier became their laughter, the more raucous their jokes, the redder their faces. It was if all the woes and disappointments they might have quietly lamented at the start of the evening, had now dissolved into nothingness, leaving only heartiness of spirit and goodwill to all in their place.

'I must go down to the cellar,' said Will, at half past nine.

Not for the first time in the evening, and not for the last, replenishments needed to be brought up.

'Right,' said Jessie, a short time later, taking off her apron. 'I think that's me done. I've left you two some stew, and there's some for Will. If anyone wants anything else, they'll have to cook it themselves.' And with that, she was off on her way home.

At ten o'clock both rooms were as full as they had been at nine o'clock, and it was only as the clock crept on towards eleven that the company began to thin out. Vicky was collecting the last mugs and Anna was wiping the tables when the slamming of the front door announced the return of Abel Slattery. If he was drunk it did not appear in any stumbling or unsteadiness of foot, but there was a look in his eye and a curled smile on his lips that spoke of a desire for mischief.

'Come here, wench!' he commanded, clicking his finger and thumb in Anna's direction. 'It's time you learned to put a little warmth in your welcome.'

'Take the pots to the kitchen, Vicky,' she called without looking up from her task. 'Don't be afraid.'

'Don't be afraid,' Abel Slattery mimicked, with a harsh laugh. 'And you, mistress, don't forget who puts a roof over your head and feeds you. Now, come here, as I tell you.'

'If my father knew how you treated me, he'd have you before the magistrate.'

At this, Abel Slattery gave another coarse laugh. 'Your father! If it was up to your father, you'd be out on the street, hussy, that's where you would be.'

Setting her tray down in the kitchen, and realising that her hands were quivering with fear, Vicky heard Abel Slattery bark out his order a third time, and then there was the sound of a scuffle. Rushing back to the door, she saw that he had grasped Anna by the throat of her dress, and, twisting it in one hand, was lifting her up so that her face was level with his.

'Now, slattern,' he hissed, 'what have you to say for yourself?'

By way of answer, Anna made the action of spitting in his face, and found herself, in return, flung across the room, taking with her several stools, and upending a table, before landing with her back against the bar. Then, before she had time to recover from the shock, Abel Slattery had followed her, and grasping her again, this time by her hair behind, had lifted her up onto her feet, and then pulled back on her hair, so that she was on her tiptoes but arched backwards.

'A bit of spirit, have we, then!' he mocked. 'I like a bit of spirit. Let's see where it gets us, shall we!'

Anna let out a cry of pain as he drew her towards the door, pushing Vicky aside as he did so, but just then, laboured footsteps were heard on the cellar steps, and Will appeared behind the bar. There was a moment of silence, as he took in the scene in his usual slow and unspoken way, but there was perhaps just enough of a threat in his bulky presence to make Abel Slattery think again about his next action.

'Enough of this nonsense,' he said, freeing Anna and letting her regain her balance. 'Pour me a brandy, Will. We'll leave this sport for another day.'

Anna hurried through to the kitchen, followed by Vicky. Then Anna led the way upstairs, to their chamber. There, beneath her apron, she revealed the long kitchen knife she had brought with her. 'Let him try to disturb our sleep tonight,' she said, 'and this is for him.'

16

～

Robert and Lucy were waiting for Vicky to finish her tale. They were sitting before the fire in Granny Matty's parlour. Vicky had walked over there, slipping out of the Sun Inn as soon as the daylight was full. Granny was busy at some task in the kitchen. Matty himself, not really part of the group, but as interested as anyone else, was hovering at the door, listening.

'And did he?' asked Lucy, at last, her eyes wide with disbelief.

'Did he what?'

'Disturb your sleep.'

Vicky shook her head. 'We lay awake for a long time, listening, but it all stayed quiet. He must have had some more brandy and gone to bed.'

'Thank goodness for that!' said Lucy. 'What does he look like?'

'Slattery? Ugly.'

'What do you mean, ugly?' asked Robert.

'He gives me the creeps.'

'Yes, but slugs give you the creeps, lots of things give you the creeps. What exactly do you mean?'

'I don't know. Just creepy.'

'Describe him.'

Vicky thought for a moment. 'Big,' she said at last.

'How do you mean? Fat?'

'Not exactly fat.'

'Is he tall?'

'Maybe tall. All grown-ups seem tall to me.'

'How old?'

'Gosh. No idea really.'

'Older than dad?'

'Maybe the same. Maybe a bit younger.'

'How else is he different from dad?'

'Apart from his clothes?'

'Yes, obviously.'

'Well, dad doesn't have a scruffy beard, or eyebrows that cross over. Or a nasty look about his mouth. Or a boil on his neck.'

'Has he got a boil on his neck?'

'Yes.'

'Yuk,' said Lucy.

They sat in silence for some time.

'What do you think we should do?' asked Vicky, at last, looking towards Robert.

'I don't know if there is anything we can do,' said Robert. 'Tomorrow is Christmas Day, and you know what that means, don't you?'

'Is that when I get my light thing?' asked Matty. This was ignored by the others.

'The thing is.' Vicky continued, 'what will happen to her once we've gone? Now I've seen it myself, I know how dangerous he is.'

'Could we take her with us, maybe?' asked Lucy, uncertainly.

Robert's face took on a troubled look. 'I don't know if it would work like that,' he said. 'I mean, we don't even know if it will work for us. It's just guesswork really.'

'What about the power of imagination?' asked Lucy. 'Didn't you say it was all down to that?'

'I think it is. But I don't have all the answers. Tell me again, Vicky, what did she say about her father?'

'That he would have Abel Slattery up before the magistrate.'

'And how did he react?'

'He just mocked her.'

Again, they sat for some time in silence.

'I suppose,' said Robert, finally, 'if we could get some sort of message to her father in Alnwick, he might do something. I mean if he really knew what was going on.'

'Can't we try that then?'

'It's about four miles. That's eight miles altogether. I suppose we could manage that. But the other thing is, we don't know exactly when the storm is going to be. Only that it is on Christmas Day. That could be, you know, tomorrow, or tomorrow night, or it could be just after midnight tonight. That could be cutting it fine if anything happens, I mean if we get delayed at all.'

'We could go on horseback,' said Lucy, suddenly. 'That would be much quicker.'

'But how could we do that?'

'Abel Slattery's horse is in the stables at the farm, just along from here. Remember, I went there and talked to Tom, the farmer. I could say I've been sent with a message to saddle the horse up, and then bring him away. I'm sure Tom would do it.'

'But who is going to go?' asked Robert. 'I don't know how to ride a horse.'

'No, but I do,' said Lucy.

'But you can't go,' said Robert. 'Not on your own.'

'You'd have to go with her, Robert,' said Vicky. 'Can you get two people on a saddle, Lucy?'

'I suppose so, yes. A horse can carry a heavy man. Robert's bigger than me, but I weigh hardly anything at all, really, not as far as a horse is concerned.'

'What do you think, then, Robert?'

Robert seemed to be weighing it all up in his mind, as if there were all sorts of unknown factors to be considered. They waited.

'OK,' he said, in the end. 'I suppose we could give it a go.'

'What shall I do?' asked Vicky. 'Shall I stay here?'

'It might be safer,' suggested Lucy.

'Actually,' said Robert, after giving it some thought, 'it might be better if you went back. He's not got it in for you, and the more things seem normal, the less chance there is that he'll suspect something's going on.'

'OK,' said Vicky, a little uncertainly.

'Besides, you can tell Anna what's going on. At least she'll know we're trying to do something to help her. Also, if we are to make our getaway tonight, I mean, if the storm looks like breaking after midnight, it might be useful if she could get our normal clothes ready.'

The room fell silent again. Everyone seemed to have agreed that the plan was set, and that now it was a matter of putting it all into practice.

17

An hour later, Lucy found herself once again passing along the track that led up between the outbuildings into the farmyard. There was no immediate sign of Tom, so she waited by a corner, in the shadow. Ten minutes passed and then another five. A woman came out of the door of the farmhouse with a bucket. Lucy stepped further back into the shadow. Two minutes later the woman came back again and went into the farmhouse. That must be Jessie, she thought to herself, Tom's wife.

It might well be, she reflected, that Tom was working on some remote part of the farm today, in which case he might not be back until later, possibly much later. She weighed this up for a time, hoping that he might simply turn round a corner at any moment and appear in the farmyard, and then, making her mind up, she went across the yard and knocked on the farmhouse door.

The top half of the door opened, and the woman appeared. 'I wondered how long you'd stand out there in the cold for, hen. I thought maybe your feet were frozen to the cobbles.'

'I'm sorry,' said Lucy, embarrassed that she had been watched all along, 'I didn't want to disturb you. I just wanted a word with Tom, and I hoped he might be about.'

'Oh, you did, did you? And what sort of word might you be wanting with him, then.'

'It's about a horse.'

'Oh aye?'

'Yes, it's about Abel Slattery's horse.'

'Oh aye, so you'll be the lass who came the other day asking about Abel Slattery's horse, then?'

'Yes.'

The woman nodded her head a few times as if she was trying to put a picture together. 'Why don't you sit down for a minute, hen. Sit by the fire a minute if you like.'

'Do you think he'll be long?'

The woman tilted her head one way, then the other. 'He'll come in when he comes in, and that'll be when the work's done. That's how it is on a farm.'

'Only the thing is, I'm in a bit of a rush, you see.'

'You'll take a cup of tea, maybe, while you're waiting.'

The woman went to a stove, and lifted a blackened pot, pouring boiled water into another pot. Lucy sat by the fire and warmed her hands, thinking of Robert, waiting, as they had agreed, at the top of the lane. Then the woman approached, with a mug, and put it into Lucy's hands. Then she sat down herself.

'Perhaps you'd better tell me what this is all about, hen.'

'It's difficult to explain,' said Lucy.

'If you know Abel Slattery at all, you'll perhaps know that it's best to keep well clear of him, especially a young lass like you. He keeps his horse here from time to time, but he's no friend of ours. You'd do well not to get involved with him.'

'I'm not involved with him. In fact, to tell you the whole truth, I've never met him, but a friend of mine knows Anna, who keeps the inn and the house for him, and has told me how badly he treats her, and I need to get to Alnwick to get a message to her father, if I can find him, in the hope that he will come and take her back home with him.'

'And that's why you want Abel Slattery's horse, then?'

'Yes. You see, well, we have to get away tonight, me and my friends, and it would take a long time to walk to Alnwick and back, and you see, I can ride. I mean, I know how to ride a horse.'

'It's a cold day for a jaunt on horseback, hen.'

'I don't mind that. Really. I'm quite used to being cold.'

The woman laughed, as if amused by Lucy's simplicity. 'Here,' she said, lifting a cloak from a hook on the back of a door. 'Wear this. Now, do you know how to saddle a horse?'

'Yes,' Lucy replied. 'I think so. Only I might need a little help lifting the saddle into place.'

'Come along then.'

The woman led the way from the farmhouse to the stable, and together they managed the tackle and prepared Gimlet for a ride. Lucy led him to the cobbles of the farmyard, and then, placing her foot in the stirrup, she thrust herself up into the saddle. Nervously at first, she led him to the gate, and then, seeing that he was compliant to the reins, she pricked him on into a trot.

Robert was waiting at the corner of the lane, as they had arranged.

'You've been a while,' he said.

'Sorry. Tom wasn't there. I had to persuade Jessie, that's his wife, to help me.'

'So, what do I do, then?'

'I'll take my foot out of this stirrup. You put your foot in and hitch up. You can grab the back of the saddle. I can help you too. Then just try to swing your other leg over.'

Robert tried this two or three times without success, unable to combine the mixture of force and balance required to complete the action.

'Maybe it would be easier if I got off first,' Lucy suggested.

'I'll just give it one more go.'

Robert put his foot in the stirrup once more, concentrated for a moment, and then pushed. Lucy caught hold of one arm and pulled, and this time he managed to swing his free leg over the horse's back, though now it took both a moment's effort to prevent him toppling over on the other side.

'I think I'm on,' he said, when the laughter of the incident had passed.

'Right,' said Lucy, 'I'll have to have the stirrup back. There's nothing for you to hold onto, so you'll have to put your arms round my waist.'

'Yes, all right,' said Robert, necessity overcoming embarrassment.

'It's a bit of a squeeze. Are you ready?'

'Ready.'

She pulled on the rein a little and Gimlet walked on.

'Are you OK?' she called.

'Yes,' Robert replied.

They came to the Mount Pleasant area, above the village, without seeing anyone, and then took the path down to the river's edge.

'Over there is where the bridge will be when they build it,' said Robert. 'Remember what Anna said, that we could ford the river near here.'

'It looks quite shallow. Gimlet seems to know where he is. Shall we try it?'

'OK.'

A minute later, they were across the river finding the path on the far bank.

'Do you know the way now?' asked Lucy.

'We need to go past Lesbury. I know that. That's where the modern road is.'

'Which way is Lesbury?'

'Just keep going on this path, I think.'

Sure enough, after fifteen minutes, a church tower came into view, and at the foot of it, the small village of Lesbury. Here the river had swept back in a curve, but a narrow stone bridge allowed them to cross.

'This is the place where the eighteen arches are,' said Robert suddenly.

'The what?'

'The eighteen arches. On the road from Alnwick to Alnmouth. It's a viaduct they built for the railway when that came along.'

'Right. If we ever get back, you can show me.'

'Yes. I will.'

They rode on, for another fifteen minutes and then stopped, where there was a water trough at the edge of a field, to give Gimlet a rest.

'Do you think we'll be able to find it when we get there? The place where Anna's father lives?'

'She said he was a wine merchant,' Robert replied. 'I think she said it was near the centre of the town. That shouldn't be too difficult to find.'

'Let's hope not. Are you ready?'

They mounted the horse again, this time with Robert going first and Lucy following, which proved easier to arrange. The sky had grown noticeably darker since the start of the journey, however, and they had gone not more than half a mile further, when a sudden heavy downpour of rain forced them to take shelter beneath the boughs of a large oak tree in the corner of a wood.

'What's happening with your parents, at home?' asked Robert, as they waited for it to ease off. 'Mum said something. Do you mind me asking?'

Lucy shrugged her shoulders. 'They are supposed to be sorting something out. Which means that they'll probably be getting divorced.'

'So what do you think will happen to you?'

'I don't know. That's probably part of what they're sorting out.'

'It happens to a lot of people. I know a few people whose parents have separated or divorced. It's just life, I suppose.'

'It's still not easy, though.'

'Sorry if I was, you know, off with you at the start of the holiday.'

'It's all right. I know I was a bit of a drip. Talking of which...'

Robert grinned. The rain was now finding its way through the branches of the tree under which they were trying to find shelter. 'Perhaps we'd better just risk it,' he said.

They set off again. The rain eased off slightly for a time, but then suddenly redoubled its force. Luckily this time, they found themselves near a rough shepherd's hut in the corner of a field, set against a hedge and with posts that held up a sloping roof. It was not entirely waterproof, but it kept the worst of the rain off their heads.

'What do you think of Anna?' asked Robert, for conversation, as they waited.

'She's really nice. I like her. Isn't it funny that she can't read, though?'

'To us, maybe. But I suppose most people couldn't... can't, whichever way you put it.'

'Do you like her?' asked Lucy.

'Yes. I'd be sorry if anything bad happened to her. You know, after we go. I really like her.'

There was an awkward pause, as if Robert had said more than he intended. 'Don't know what we would have done without her really,' he added, striking a more practical note. 'It's funny, isn't it?' he went on. 'If we get back, I mean to our own time, and if she really existed, she would have been dead for probably a hundred and fifty years.'

'That's spooky,' said Lucy.

'Unless all things are happening all the time.'

'How do you mean?'

'It's something I think about sometimes. If time is just a kind of illusion and there's no such thing as history because all things are happening all the time.'

'That's spooky too.'

They waited another ten minutes for the rain to slacken and then set out again.

'I've been thinking,' said Robert, 'when we get to Alnwick, it's best we get off the horse and walk. Less likely to draw attention that way. Then, if we find out where Anna's father lives, one of us will have to look after the horse while the other tries to talk to him.'

'You'd be better than me at that,' said Lucy. 'I'll look after Gimlet. Is that all right?'

It was not much further until they came within sight of a tall stone archway straddling the road, linked to the walls which surrounded the town.

'Hotspur's Tower,' said Robert.

'What?'

'That's what they call it. Hotspur's Tower. He was a chap in the old days. I mean, the very old days. I think he lived at Warkworth. Bit of a character, my dad says.'

'Maybe,' suggested Lucy, 'next time we go into a time warp, we might meet up with him.'

Dismounting, they led Gimlet through the arch, onto a street which spread downwards on a slight slope into the town. There were some stalls by the side of the street, and sufficient people coming and going about their business for them not to feel too noticeable. They continued to the foot of the town. From here they could see, as the street rose again, another arched gate – the end of the town.

'Do you remember it at all?' asked Lucy.

'Vaguely,' Robert replied. 'It's changed a lot. I think if we turn up there, we'll come to the castle. And after that, it's just open country and the river again.'

'I haven't seen a wine merchant's anywhere.'

'No, nor me. I wish we'd asked Anna to give us directions now.'

'We'll have to ask someone.'

On the other side of the street was an inn yard, and as they deliberated, a man entered on horseback, dismounted, and handed the horse on to another who looked as if he was in charge of the yard.

'I've got an idea,' said Robert. 'Wait here.'

He led Gimlet across into the yard.

'How much to look after the horse for an hour?' he asked, as the ostler approached.

'Tuppence for you, young squire.'

'It's not for me, but for my master, who has some business in the town. But here's your tuppence. Tell me, there is a wine merchant here with the name of Summers, can you direct me to his premises?'

It was not far from where they now were, but the shop and its doorway were a little way up an obscure alleyway whose entrance they had passed some minutes before. They stood before the door, which was at the top of three steps with a short iron railing To the side was a brass plate with the inscription: *E. Summers, Purveyor of Fine Wines and Spirits.* They glanced at each other, as if summoning the courage to knock and at last Robert stood on the first step, lifted the brass knocker, and gave two short taps, then stepped back to the pavement.

'What will we do if *she* answers?' asked Lucy in a hushed voice. 'You know, Anna's stepmother.'

'I don't know,' Robert replied. 'Haven't thought that far.'

Half a minute passed, and nothing happened. 'Perhaps they aren't in,' said Robert.

'Shall we try again? I'll do it this time.'

Lucy stepped up, lifted the brass knocker, and made four taps, in a little rhythm, slightly louder than Robert's had been.

A short time later, the sounds of a sliding bolt and a key turning in a lock were heard, and the door opened to reveal a young man in a black frock coat, white knee breeches and socks, and a white cravat, who informed them, in a polite and practised voice, that business had finished for the day and would not resume until the second day after Christmas.

He then looked ready to close the door without further ado, but Robert quickly excused himself to say that it was not wine business but family business that had brought them here, and to ask if they might be permitted to speak to Mr Summers.

The young man, who seemed by his manner and dress to be a servant or an employee, looked them both up and down with a quick glance, and then, after a moment of thought, stepped back to let them come through the door into a long hall with black and white tiles on the floor and walls of deep crimson. There was a faint smell which reminded Robert of the fumes of brandy he and Matty had smelled aboard the Merry Joan, but this was more refined and could have been mixed with the smell of other spirits, possibly tobacco.

Half way along the corridor was a glass panelled door which evidently led into the shop, for shelves and racks of bottles and casks were visible as they passed. A couple of steps further, another door opened into a small room with a leather topped table and chairs which - with its ledgers, quills and inkwells - seemed to be an office. The young man ushered them into this room and told them, in his soft formal voice, that they were to wait there.

He then disappeared.

'So far, so good,' said Robert under his breath.

'Fingers crossed!'

They waited in silence until, perhaps three minutes later, a sound of shuffling became audible, as of slippers moving along the tiles, and the door opened again.

The man who now appeared, though not an old man, had a slight stoop of the shoulders, thinning hair streaked with grey and a pale complexion; he wore gold rimmed spectacles with small half-moon lenses, and behind them his eyes seemed red and watery, as if he had a cold or some other irritation. It seemed to Robert that the expression of his face was anxious, almost fretful, but there was also something about the over-all composition of his features that reminded him, quite unmistakeably, of Anna.

'John tells me you have some business with me,' he said, in a dry husky voice, 'of a personal nature.'

'It's about Anna,' said Robert.

'Who?'

'Your daughter, Anna.'

For a moment, the man's face remained impassive, as if he might be intending to deny all knowledge of an Anna who might be his daughter. Then his expression changed to one of pain, and he reached for the arm of a chair to help lower himself into the seat. He took out a handkerchief, took off his spectacles, and wiped his eyes. Then, after a moment of com-posing himself, and replacing his spectacles, he asked, 'Are you friends of Anna?'

'Yes,' replied Lucy, in a little voice. 'I'm Lucy and this is Robert, and we are Anna's friends. From Alnmouth.'

'Alnmouth, yes,' said the man. 'And is she happy? Is she settled? Have you come with a message from her?'

Robert and Lucy exchanged looks.

'I'm afraid to say,' said Robert, trying to tread carefully with his words, 'that she is not at all settled and not at all happy.'

'That's what we've come to tell you,' said Lucy.

The man seemed to ponder this in a way which suggested it was a truth he already knew, or suspected, but did not wish to face up to. For a moment it seemed that every ounce of life and energy had drained out of him. 'But she is in a good position,' he said, rallying a little, 'an excellent position for a young woman, and perhaps, eventually, Mr Slattery will take her as his wife, and then her future will be secure.'

'Mr Slattery is very cruel to her,' said Lucy.

'He is abusive towards her,' said Robert, not sure which words or phrases would express his meaning to a person living in 1806. 'He strikes her, especially when he is drunk. She lives in fear of his threats. He treats her as a slave.'

Mr Summers stared as Robert finished, then closed his eyes firmly and let out a long breath. 'This is not as it should be,' he muttered, as if talking only to himself. 'Not as it should be at all, and yet what can I do?'

'Can't you let her come back here?' asked Robert.

Mr Summers looked up, and then, again as if speaking for his own benefit, said, 'Impossible. Impossible. As things stand. Quite impossible.'

'It may be that her life is in danger,' said Robert.

'No,' said Mr Summers, standing up suddenly and banging his fist on the table, 'I will hear no more of this.'

Then, just as suddenly, he sat down again, sinking into the chair with an air of despair.

'What shall we tell her?' asked Robert.

'You will tell her nothing,' came another voice, sharp and commanding. It was a woman's voice, and as she spoke the owner of the voice came into doorway. She was a small woman, younger than Mr Summers by some years, with dark hair set in ringlets on each side of a cap with a real lace border, a prominent and imposing nose, reddened lips, and piercing blue eyes. She wore a purple blouse, with black trim and lacework and a high collar, and full dark skirts. 'You will tell her nothing,' she repeated, this time almost a hiss. 'The only message is that she should be grateful with what kindness has provided for her. And if you must tell her something, tell her this, that Abel Slattery shall know of it if she chooses to send such a pack of wicked lies, with such as you, here ever again.'

'They're not lies,' said Lucy, her lip quivering on the verge of tears. Robert took hold of her hand.

'They aren't lies,' he repeated, as boldly as he dare.

The woman's face creased into a bitter scowl, her eyes flashing with anger, her bottom lip pushed out like a crushed cherry.

'Get out!' she hissed. 'Get out of this house, before...'

She did not finish this threat but stepped out of the door, and called, almost shrieked along the hallway, 'John! John! Come immediately and throw these vagabonds out onto the street. John, John! Do you hear me?'

Mr Summers looked to first Robert and then Lucy with eyes that seemed to be expressing a meek appeal for understanding. 'She will have her way,' he said, pitifully, 'she will have her way.'

'Can't you stand up to her?'

'Stand up to her?' said Mr Summers, with a sigh, almost a laugh, of hopelessness.

John appeared in the doorway. 'Sir?' he asked in a patient voice.

'Give me a moment, John.'

John nodded and stood to one side just outside the door.

'Tell her that I think of her often. Tell her that I am glad she has friends who care for her welfare. Tell her that perhaps, in time, I will be able to rectify the situation. Tell her that I pray that she will be granted patience.'

'Is that all?' said Robert.

Mr Summers rose from his chair and clasped Robert by the hand. 'Thank you,' he said. 'Thank you, young man, from the bottom of my heart. I know that in you she has a friend who will make sure she comes to no harm.'

And with that he turned and shuffled from the room. As he disappeared, John appeared again. 'Sir,' he said to Robert, 'Miss,' to Lucy, politely, as if they were valued customers, lifting his arm to direct them to the outer door.

'I knew she was there,' said Lucy when they were outside. 'I saw a shadow hovering there, by the door, and I guessed it was her, but I couldn't say anything.'

'Wouldn't have done any good, anyway. He's obviously terrified of her.'

'How could he have chosen such a what's it, what's the word?'

'Harridan,' suggested Robert.

'How could he have chosen such a harridan and then get rid of someone as lovely as Anna.'

'Search me.'

'What should we do next?'

'Nothing we can do. We'll just have to get Gimlet and go back. The light's already starting to fade. Remember about tonight. We need to be ready.'

'We did the best we could, didn't we?'

'Yes. I don't see that there's anything else we could have done.'

'It's funny what he said to you, wasn't it? Making sure she came to no harm.'

'He doesn't know, though, does he?'

'I suppose not.'

'How could he?'

'It makes you wonder, though.'

'Wonder what?'

'Oh nothing.'

Gimlet was waiting in the inn yard. They walked him to the town gate, and then, mounting him again, began their journey back to Alnmouth.

18

The darkness began to close in as they retraced their journey of the morning. Where it was possible, Lucy spurred Gimlet into a canter, but in places the ground was uneven, and as the shadow increased - and with it, the chance of a stumble or fall - she reined back to a trot and then to a walk. For a short time, an eerie gash of sun in the west behind them cast a strange lurid light on the path, but when it was gone the darkness seemed more intense. Before they reached the bridge in Lesbury, low rumblings of thunder could be heard in the distance, as if the storm was gathering together its forces, uncertain whether to attack or delay.

In Lesbury, they stopped for ten minutes to allow Gimlet to drink and rest, and talked about the plan for when they got back. They decided that it was best for them to stay together taking Gimlet back to the farm, and then walk into Alnmouth to meet up with Vicky and Anna.

'It's probably best if we can all meet up at the granary,' said Robert. 'The storm seems to have gone into a lull. It may be we'll have to wait until tomorrow.'

'I won't get a chance to say goodbye to Granny Matty, will I?'

'Probably best not to complicate anything. Anyway, I have a strange feeling the people we've met won't remember us at all. I think maybe it'll just seem as if we were part of a dream they had, you know, like when you wake up and you know you've had a dream, but it dissolves away in just a few seconds. Maybe it will be like that for us too.'

'How weird! Do you mean we won't even be able to talk to each other about all this?'

'Who knows? Like I said, it's all just guesswork really.'

'Are we going to tell Anna, you know, about Alnwick and seeing her father?'

'I don't know. Vicky's probably told her we were planning to go. Maybe she'll ask us.'

They mounted Gimlet once more and made their way onwards, slowly, towards the ford on the river, just above the village. Then, for the last stage of the journey, Robert walked alongside as Lucy rode. They came to the gate to the farm. Lucy dismounted and Robert waited as she led Gimlet across the yard. There was no light in the farmhouse, but as she approached, the door opened and a figure appeared in the shadow and then, silently, led the way towards the stable. At the stable door, the figure turned and took the reins from her.

'Tom?' she asked.

There was no reply. She peered into the shadow where the face should be but there were no features.

She tried to say his name again, but nothing came from her mouth, and then, realising that she could no longer breathe, she gave way to panic.

'Lucy! Lucy!'

Someone was tapping her cheek lightly, and as she came to, she realised the voice was Robert's.

'I must have fainted,' she said.

'Let's get away from here,' said Robert. 'Can you stand up?'

'I think so if you help me. Is Gimlet all right?'

Robert didn't answer.

'What's the matter?' she asked. Then, looking round, she saw that the stable building was no longer there, and that the farmhouse itself was no more than a ruin, abandoned and empty.

'What's happened?'

'Come on,' said Robert. 'Maybe we should hurry.'

He put his arm round her shoulder and guided her out from what had once been the farmyard, out onto the lane.

'I think it's beginning to fade,' he said, as they walked towards the village. 'I noticed, when you walked across the yard, there was no sound of Gimlet's hooves on the cobbles, and then, when you didn't come back, I came to look and found you just lying there, and the rest, well, you saw it for yourself.'

'When you say, it's beginning to fade, do you mean we're already partly back in our own time?'

'It could be. We need to find Vicky.'

'OK. I'm all right now. We can run if you like.'

Anna was waiting for them at the corner by the granary and as soon as they approached, she opened the door and ushered them in. It was clear that she was in a distraught state.

'What's the matter?' asked Robert.

'You shouldn't have gone!' she said, with anguish in her voice. 'You should never have gone. If you'd have asked me, I would have told you, no good could possibly come of it. Worse.'

'We were trying to help you,' said Lucy, tearful.

'What help did you think you could possibly be?' Anna insisted.

'Worse?' asked Robert. 'What did you mean by worse'?'

'You should have known better than to let Matty overhear your plans. Have you not learned by now how untrustworthy he is?'

'Why, what has he done?'

'He came here to see Abel Slattery. He told him the whole thing. He said that you were going to Alnwick to see my father, and that you were going to come back here for Vicky - he told him Vicky was your sister - and then you were all going to go to Berwick to report the cargo of the Merry Joan to the Excise there.'

'But that's ridiculous!'

'He told him that you forced him to go out to the Merry Joan with you, and that you lifted the hatch and saw what was in the hold.'

'We did go there, but it was Matty's idea, not mine.'

'It makes no difference. Abel Slattery believed him.'

'We'd better get Vicky,' said Lucy.

'Yes,' said Robert faintly. 'If we're going to go tonight, or tomorrow, we need to be ready. Maybe we should just go straight to Woden's Hill and wait there.'

'Can you go and tell her, Anna. Bring her here.'

'I can't bring her here,' said Anna. 'That's what I meant by worse, Robert. Abel Slattery has taken her to the Merry Joan. Forced her to go with him. As a hostage. To warn you to leave things be.'

'But surely he could have just warned us here.'

'I can't speak for him. He was in a rage. Like a madman. God only knows what he is capable of.'

A dreadful silence fell in the room.

'There's only one thing for it,' said Robert, at last. 'We'll have to go. Out to the Merry Joan, I mean. We've got to try to rescue her.'

'That may make him even more desperate,' said Anna. 'Perhaps you should wait until tomorrow, to see if he calms down. Maybe he'll see sense and just bring her back.'

'But what if we haven't got until tomorrow?' asked Robert.

Chapter 19

19

Thunder was again tumbling around the edges of the dark sky, seeming to belong to no one part of it, patrolling the horizon, roving about restlessly, unable to decide on a place to settle. Occasionally a faint distant lightning flickered, as if tangled electrical wires were short-circuiting.

Leading the way, Robert followed the path down to the shore, with Lucy and Anna just behind. Anna had been trying to persuade him not to venture on this escapade, but his mind was set.

The rowing boats and cobles had been drawn as far up the beach as possible, but the rising tide was already lapping towards them. Robert stepped through and chose one he thought he would be able to manage and began to untie it from its post.

'You stay here with Anna,' he said, turning back to Lucy.

'Yes,' Anna agreed, putting her arm around Lucy's shoulder. 'It will be safer for you here.'

'No!' Lucy protested. 'Whatever happens we have to try to stay together.'

Anna closed her arms round Lucy as if to hold her back, but Lucy broke free. 'I'm coming with you, Robert,' she insisted.

She stepped into the little boat as Robert pushed it fully into the water. Then he jumped in after her, and sitting down on the transom, manipulated the oars into position.

'I'll fetch a lamp, and wait here,' called Anna. 'For when you're coming back.'

As Robert pulled away, he could just make out the form of Anna disappearing up the alley back towards the Sun Inn and the Granary.

'Do you know where to go?' asked Lucy.

'I think so. It's true that I went out to the Merry Joan with Matty a couple of days ago. It was proper daylight then, though.'

A cold gusty breeze was now coming across the estuary towards them. Robert recalled how Matty had used the wind and the current to pull round onto the far side of the Merry Joan, where the ladder was, and tried to follow the same line but it was not easy, and besides there were now waves on the current which slapped against the side of the boat, rocking it and sending cold spray over them.

'Can you see her?' asked Robert.

'I think so. The big one with two masts?'

In fact, it was not difficult to pick out the Merry Joan, as all the other boats had pulled in as close to the shore as they could.

'Are there any lights on board?' he said, glancing over his shoulder.

'Yes. There's some kind of light on the deck. Like a lantern.'

Now in a steady rhythm, Robert pulled the oars easily, and began to angle the course towards the mooring of the Merry Joan. Ten minutes later they were standing next to its hull with the ladder hanging above.

'I'll go first,' said Robert, tying the boat up as he had seen Matty do. 'You stay here, if you like.'

'No, I'll come with you. Well, I'll do my best.'

Robert stepped onto the ladder, remembering the way it swayed, and trying not to be put off. Step by step, he climbed up to the rail, and beckoned Lucy to follow. As she got close, he reached his hand under her arm and helped her over the rail.

'What now?' she whispered.

'There's nobody about. Maybe, just try to explore, see if we can find where Vicky is.'

Robert led the way along the deck to the cabin where he and Matty had seen the two drunken men who were supposed to be on watch. It was possible, he thought, that if Abel Slattery had confined her there, they could release her and get away without being noticed.

As they approached, there was a sudden flash of lightning and then after the six seconds which Robert counted, a crack of thunder, much nearer now. Then, the door of the cabin opened, and there stood Abel Slattery, with Vicky in front of him, grasped in his left arm. Behind them, holding a lantern in one hand and a pistol in the other, was Matty.

'Point the gun at the boy,' commanded Abel Slattery, 'in case he tries anything. Then put the lantern where all can see.'

Matty pointed the gun towards Robert and set the lantern on a hook on the wall of the fo'c'sle. In the light which it now cast, Robert could see that, in his right hand, Abel Slattery was holding a knife, and that the knife was trained on Vicky's throat, so that one simple stroke would be enough to slice it open.

Robert froze. In all his imaginings of adventure, he had always thought he would know what to do if a situation like this cropped up: the quick daring reaction, the decisive counterthrust.

The truth was he wasn't up to it. His stomach was sick and faint. He could not do anything. He was weak and frightened.

'Take them down into the hold,' said Abel Slattery. 'Let the little girl go first, then the boy. Make sure you keep the gun on his back. I'll bring this one.'

'Best do as he says,' said Matty, indicating the direction to follow.

As Robert moved, Matty edged cautiously round, as if to keep a distance between them.

And then a shot rang out.

Lucy screamed. Startled, Robert dropped to his knees. Then, glancing up, he saw that a dark circular stain had appeared on Abel Slattery's brow.

For a moment he looked shocked.

For another moment he looked resentful.

Then, letting Vicky go, he fell slowly forward onto the deck. Whimpering, Vicky scrambled across the deck and fell on Robert, squeezing her arms around his neck.

Turning his head, Robert saw Matty, the pistol - with smoke still rising from its barrel - in his lifted right hand.

Lucy, frozen, held her hands to her face, pale as that of a ghost.

'Come on, quickly,' called Robert, finding the power to act at last. He guided first Vicky and then Lucy to the ladder and watched them down. Then he turned to face Matty.

'I think he was going to kill you,' said Matty. 'All three of you. Probably me too. He knew you would come after Vicky. He was going to lock you in the hold, until the brandy was unloaded. He struck a deal with Erskine. I heard them talking.'

'But what would be the point of killing us?'

'Because he thought you were going to make trouble. That was my fault. I made it up. I don't know why. I was trying to get into his good books, I suppose. I didn't know it would lead to this.'

'What are you going to do?'

'I don't know.'

'Come with us.'

'I've just killed him,' said Matty, as if a terrible reality had just dawned on him.

'You had to. He would have killed Vicky.'

'Only because I told him stuff. It's my fault really.'

'He was a bad man. He deserved it.'

'Maybe. You go. I have to think what to do.'

Robert climbed over the rail, and looked back to where Matty was standing.

'Here,' he said, reaching into his jerkin. He pulled out the mobile phone and switched on the torch. 'It won't last long, but it's yours now.'

Matty stepped forward and took the phone. 'Thanks,' he said, the ghost of a smile on his lips.

'Matty killed him,' said Lucy, as Robert sculled the little boat towards the shore.

'No, he didn't,' said Robert. 'It's just a game.'

'He killed Abel Slattery.'

'There's no such person as Abel Slattery,' said Robert. 'I understand it now. I made it all up. In my imagination. I don't know how, but I managed to pull you two into it, to make you believe it was all real.'

'What about Anna?'

'There's no such person as Anna, either.'

Lucy fell silent, as if too shocked and confused to say more. Robert sculled on, with the wind now blustering around their ears and whipping up spray from the waves of the high tide.

'If there's no such person as Anna,' Lucy called, at last, 'Who is that then?'

Standing on the shore, in the pale light of the lantern she was holding, was, quite unmistakably, the figure of Anna.

'You need your clothes,' she said, as they stepped out of the tender onto the sand. 'Come quickly. To the corn store. You have to change into your own clothes. Then you must hurry. There is no time to lose.'

As she said this, a flash of lightning crossed the sky, illuminating for a moment the ghostly shadow of the ship from which they had just escaped. Then, a few seconds later, came a sudden violent crash of thunder.

Robert changed quickly into his shorts and T-shirt and came down to the door where Anna was waiting.

'I wish we didn't have to leave you here,' he said.

'I can't come with you. You know that, don't you?'

'Yes.'

'Is it in your power to stay?'

'I don't know.'

'Would you, if you could?'

'I have to think about my sister and Lucy.'

'Yes. Of course, you do.'

There was a long pause between them, one which seemed to hold a thousand questions.

Then came another flash of jagged lightning across the sky and an immediate crash of thunder.

'It's nearly overhead,' said Robert, as the steady rain turned to a sudden deluge.

Lucy and Vicky came out of the granary.

'I have to take them as far as the ferry, the church, I mean.'

'Yes,' said Anna, quietly.

As they made their way through the village, the rain was spattering noisily off the cobbles of the street and from the rooftops. The street itself was empty. Everyone had taken shelter. As they hurried along, a loud explosion came from their right. For a moment it seemed as if it was another crash of thunder, but then, across the estuary, deep red and gold flames could be seen, along the deck of the Merry Joan, with tongues licking up its masts and its rigging. They stopped to watch for a moment.

'Look at the river,' said Vicky.

'It's never been so high,' said Anna, who had followed them, a few paces behind.

'Quick,' said Robert, with panic in his voice. 'I think I know what's going to happen.'

They broke into a run until at last they reached the lowest part of the village. Ahead, the flat sandy meadow with its patches of sea grass and scrub stretched to the trickle of a brook, with Church Hill looming above. Vicky and Lucy ran ahead, clambering up onto the first slope.

'Go on,' Robert shouted, above the wind and the rain.

'Go to where the tent is. You'll be safe there.'

He turned to look back. Anna was standing no more than six feet away from him. She raised a hand in a forlorn wave, as the rain streamed over her face.

'I'll just see them safe,' he said, feeling, at the same moment, a rush of water over his shoes. Looking up, he saw that the water in the lagoon, gleaming in the light of the burning furnace of The Merry Joan, was like a rim at the top of a dam. Another flash of lightning confirmed the danger.

'Run!' screamed Vicky. 'It's going to break through...' Whatever she might have been going to add was lost in the crash of thunder. The storm was now directly above them.

Robert turned again towards Anna. She had now dropped her hand and was stepping slowly backwards.

Her lips formed a single word. He could not hear it but he knew the word was 'go'.

In an agony of indecision, Robert stood in what was soon to be, as he knew, the centre of the ferry, and now the water was cascading past him, bringing with it stones, gravel and muddy debris that rushed against his shins, nearly knocking him over. At last, he turned towards the hill, where Vicky and Lucy were clinging to each other in terror and made his decision. A moment later, above the sound of the wind, came a kind of cracking noise and then a deep growl, as tons of sand roared down the channel in a deluge of water.

20

The next day's television news carried the story of the search-and-rescue operation for a fourteen-year-old boy believed to have been caught in the outgoing tidal current of the River Aln – a notoriously dangerous spot - and swept out to sea. The bulletin showed a helicopter from the Air-Sea Rescue, scrambled to take part in the search which had been going on in the daylight hours for twenty-four hours. There was an interview with the Bosun of the Amble Lifeboat crew, who expressed his regret that the person missing had not been recovered alive, and though he didn't say so in so many words, the implication was that hope was now fading. The parents of the missing boy had asked that the press and media should allow them privacy in this time of terrible grief.

21

⌘

Afterword

Letter from Vicky Mattison to Lucy Hart

Dear Lucy,

Thanks so much for your letter. It was so nice to hear from you. As you have reminded me, it is almost twenty years since that fateful holiday we shared in Alnmouth. And now, there are you, in California, with your beautiful little family, and here am I, still in England, and still waiting for Mr Right to come along [though more of that later!].

In answer to your question, yes, the grieving for Robert was very intense, especially for my parents, and the fact that his body was never recovered made it very difficult for them to get any closure. After a few months, things began to get back to normal, though for them it was a normal with a huge hole in the middle, and I don't think things could ever actually be properly normal for them.

For me, of course, it was different, and you will understand - in part at least - the reason why. Do you remember the strange looks people gave us when we tried to explain what had really happened to the three of us? Everybody was so kind, but obviously they thought that we were making up a story to protect ourselves from facing the terrible accident that had taken place, or that we had simply become hysterical. Of course, only you and I know the truth of it: we didn't need to make anything up when we were simply saying what had actually happened.

So, my grief was different from theirs. I missed Robert badly, as you can imagine – he was my elder brother and I relied on him for almost everything, even though, as you probably remember, he could be very bossy at times. But I didn't grieve for him in the way that you would for someone who had died, and though we haven't spoken of this for a long time - hardly ever at all - you are the only person who knows why, or at least, the only person to believe it!

The last thing I remember, when the storm was at its height, and when you and I were huddled together on Church Hill, just before the river broke through, was seeing Robert standing below us with the water just coming up to the height of his knees. And Anna was just further off, waving. Do you remember that I shouted out to Robert, to tell him to hurry, to warn him of the danger? It is still so clear in my mind even after all these years. I can picture it now. He looked up towards us, and then, quite deliberately, he walked back to where Anna was standing, just as the torrent was surging through, and together - with him pulling her by the hand - they hurried back towards the village. I remember that terrified as we were, you and I made it back and found the tent just as we had left it. We clung to each other, shivering until the storm had passed, and then, when we came out, it seemed just like a normal summer day.

Needless to say, there were no more holidays to Alnmouth for our family after that. The pain, always raw, would have been too great for my parents. Mainly, when we did start going on holiday again, it was abroad, to places drenched in the sun, like Corfu and Majorca, where you could pretend to forget. Eventually, my parents divorced – it was just after I finished at university – and I think it was the best thing for them. Both of them found new partners, and I think that finally helped them to turn over a new page and leave the past behind.

I said earlier that I had still to find Mr Right, and that is true, though my present boyfriend, Simon, ticks some of the boxes, so who knows... watch this space! It was actually because of Simon that I finally went back to Alnmouth, a couple of months ago. He is attached to Durham

University's Archaeology Department, and they were doing some field work out on the far side of the village, the opposite side from Church Hill. He asked me to go and have a couple of days with him in the area after they'd finished the 'dig'. I didn't know how I'd react when I got there, but I said I would go, and I just decided to try to stay pretty cool about it all. Of course, I had no intention of telling Simon anything about the past, not at this stage, anyhow, but I did go to look at our cottage, though - or should I say our grain store - and other places associated with that holiday, and there were plenty of times when I was close to shedding a tear, I will admit.

Anyway, I had some time on my hands, later, whilst Simon was still winding things up, so I walked over the bridge to Lesbury, which, you may remember is just on the other side of the estuary. It's a nice enough little place, just a village, so I walked round. Didn't take me long to see what there was, so I thought I'd take a look at the church and that's how I came to be in the old graveyard. I'm not basically a morbid person but I do like looking at old graves and reading the inscriptions. I can do it for hours. Usually find myself getting sad about how much infant mortality there was in the old days, but anyway, I'd been in there for about twenty minutes when I came on an inscription that really set me wondering, and when I got your letter last week, I knew that I had to tell you about it and ask you what you think. I'd been almost all the way round – there were some workmen there cutting the grass, which was a nuisance – but finally, in a corner on the far side of the church, I found this particular grave, and I'd read the inscription over a couple of times before it dawned on me what I was reading, and honestly, my heart jumped up into my mouth. This what it said:

In memory of Robert Warrender of Alnmouth
Who died 26th May 1867
Also Anna, wife of the above
Who died 12th February 1869
Also their son, Robert
Who died 9th December 1885

Of course, Robert was Robert *Mattison* - same surname as me -

but Robert's second name was *Warrender*, after another branch of the family. Is it too much of a coincidence? Do you think it's possible that he used that name after he went back to Alnmouth on the night of the storm? And what about, *Anna, wife of the above*? Is that just another coincidence? The dates are possible – Robert was fourteen then, so he would have been 78 or something like that in 1869.

Anna would have been nearly 80.

Lucy, you must write and tell me what you think of all this. You may think I've finally gone completely loopy, but I know what I believe. And do you know something else,

Lucy: I don't think it's simply a question of believing what I want to believe either.

Who knows? Maybe if we could go to Woden's Hill again, on a very stormy day - just like on that holiday - the same thing would happen again, and then we would be able to find out for sure.

With love, Vicky.

THE END

22

About the Author

John Wheatley

John's family hails originally from Alnwick and he has many happy memories of visiting Alnmouth on holiday as a child. He has written novels set in Anglesey, in Middleton, near Manchester, where he was brought up, and in Yorkshire where he now lives. JOSS set in Middleton in the 1960s and ON WODEN'S HILL are two books he has written with a young adult/teenage audience in mind.

To find out more about John's work, visit his Amazon Author Central page:

https://www.amazon.com/author/johnwheatley

or take a look at his Facebook page: John Wheatley Author

or simply email him at johnwheatley@ymail.com

JOSS

When she is displaced to Middleton, near Manchester, England, in 1962, to stay with her strange Aunt Mary, an unhappy 13-year-old Joanna Logan, begins a diary. The diary reflects all her unanswered questions about what is happening with her parents. It also records her experience of Middleton, and the friendship she forms with Joss, the boy from down the street, who, unknown to his family, is keeping a special dog, Riverside Lad. Twenty-five years later, Joanna returns to Middleton, and discovers the secrets which lay beneath her aunt's life, secrets which she never suspected at the time.

https://www.amazon.co.uk/dp/B07HB9NWR5